A Vineyard Thanksgiving

The Vineyard Sunset Series

Katie Winters

Chapter One

Prologue

J ust after five in the evening on a particularly sunny day in late August, Lola Sheridan pressed her hands over her older cousin Charlotte Montgomery's eyes, then said, "Guess who's coming out on the boat tonight?"

Charlotte hated it when Lola played games like that. Lola was always the charismatic, loud one, and she liked to create chaos out of nothing. Still, the love Charlotte had for her fifteen-year-old cousin led her to say, "I don't know. Who?"

With that, Lola pulled her hands off of Charlotte's eyes and pointed at the dock in front of them. Lola's new boyfriend, Peter, stood next to his best friend, the handsome, broad-shouldered Jason Hamner. It was no secret among the Sheridan and Montgomery cousins that Charlotte had a pretty serious crush on Jason Hamner. They were also aware of the fact that she had been too terrified to do anything about it. They didn't let her forget it.

"Now's your chance," Lola breathed excitedly.

"I don't know," Charlotte whispered. Her throat tightened.

"You can't just let life pass you by, Charlotte," Lola said. She thought she was something of an authority on the subject, especially since her mother had died in a horrible boating accident a little over three years before. "You have to take it by the horns, you know? Get what you want."

"Did you read that in a magazine somewhere?" Charlotte asked.

Lola leaped out of Charlotte's clunky convertible and danced toward the dock, where she hung her arms around Peter's neck and gave him a tender kiss. Charlotte was nothing like Lola in terms of bravery, and she'd still never been kissed. She was already seventeen years old. According to her moodier cousin Christine, this was "borderline pathetic."

Charlotte got out of the car, looked into the back and front seats to ensure nothing of value remained, and then walked toward the other three. She wore a jean miniskirt with a yellow tank top, and her long brown curls wafted down her shoulders and back, catching in the breeze. She quietly thanked Lola for demanding that she wear eyeliner and lip gloss rather than shooting for the natural look for a little stint on the boat.

"There she is. Charlotte Montgomery herself," Peter said, grinning broadly.

"Hey," Charlotte replied. She didn't trust her tone. Did she sound cool enough to be among them? "Whose boat is that?"

The speed boat clunked against the dock and glittered in the gorgeous orange evening light.

"It's mine," Jason affirmed. "My dad just bought it."

"Wow. It's beautiful," Charlotte said. She forced her eyes to meet Jason's altogether perfect green ones. He was just as beautiful as anyone on the TV shows she watched with her sister, Claire, and maybe even more so.

What would Claire think of her now?

They got into the speedboat. Immediately, Lola ripped off her tank top to reveal her bikini beneath. Charlotte also wore a bikini; it was just what you did on Martha's Vineyard in the summertime. Still, she felt too awkward about just whipping off her shirt in front of Jason. She didn't want him to think she was easy. According to her mother, this was one of the worst things to make a boy think you were.

Lola doesn't have a mother. She can act however she wants.

The second the thoughts ran through her mind, Charlotte regretted them. It wasn't like she wished that reality on herself, not in a million years. When Aunt Anna had passed away, the entire island had shifted. Susan had run as fast as she could away from all of them. Apparently, she already had a baby and lived an entire other life. Christine had her eyes elsewhere, as well. This was so different from what Charlotte had assumed they would do. She'd thought she would have her family around her always.

Jason started the boat's engine and shot them out through the turquoise waters. His large hand across the steering wheel looked more like a man's hand than a boy's. Charlotte knew he had been dating someone back at school, but she had heard they'd broken up. Was he sad about it? Did he need to talk? Did boys ever need to talk, or were they just less emotional, made of muscle and sweat, with a love of sports?

"How was your summer, Char?" he asked suddenly.

He turned his face toward hers, and every cell in her body caught fire. They had hardly spoken, and here he was, calling her *Char*.

"It was okay," she admitted. In her mind, cool girls never got too excited about anything. "What about you?"

"Ah, you know. Dad thinks it's time I start fishing with him

3

most mornings, so I've been pretty tired. The wake-up call is four in the morning. I crash early."

"Wow. Yeah. That's intense," Charlotte said, tucking a strand of hair behind her ear.

"It really is. But there's something about the water in the mornings, you know? It's like I get to see this whole other world that other people miss because they're asleep," he said.

As they spoke, Lola and Peter fell into one another's arms and busied themselves, making out and whispering to one another. Charlotte's cheeks burned with embarrassment.

Jason eased the boat toward the western part of the island, toward the edges of the cliffs. He then turned off the engine and released the anchor toward the bottom of the ocean. Lola moved forward and shuffled through her backpack, where she found a bottle of cheap vodka. She yanked it open, sipped just a bit, then grimaced.

"It was the best I could get," she said with a shrug. "I snuck it out of the Sunrise Cove Inn Bistro."

I can't believe she did that. Uncle Wes would kill her if he knew.

"That's hilarious," Charlotte said, contrary to her actual thoughts.

Lola passed her the vodka, and Charlotte took the tiniest of sips. "Yum," she said, then made a face as the liquid burned her throat.

"It's disgusting," Lola stated. "But whatever, it works for today."

Charlotte sat next to Jason and gazed up at the cliffside, which caught the reflection of the brimming sunset. Peter and Jason talked about the football season, which was ramping up even now. Jason would be a senior, like Charlotte, while Peter would be a junior. It gave Charlotte every shade of panic to think about this being the last year of high school. What was she supposed to do after this? Did she have any useful skills at all?

After a few more sips of the vodka, Peter yanked off his t-shirt and jumped into the water. Lola removed her jean shorts and followed suit, yelping and flashing her long, beautiful hair behind her. She wrapped her arms around him and dunked him, and he threw her through the air, making her crash down below.

Jason turned back toward Charlotte and said, "Do you want to swim?"

Charlotte had always been kind of nervous in the water. It wasn't anything she could understand. She had been raised on an island, for goodness sakes, and had spent a number of days of her life on a boat.

"Sure," Charlotte said instead. "Sounds great."

Charlotte turned away from the others and removed her skirt and tank top. Then, she forced herself around and blinked at Jason. How were his abs even possible? They looked almost drawn on; they were so perfect.

"After you," he said, stretching his arm toward the water.

"No, no. I insist," she replied. "You first."

Suddenly, his eyes became electric green. He rushed toward her, gripped her waist, and then threw her in the water like Peter did with Lola. As Charlotte careened toward the waves, her body froze. Fear shot through her. The second she entered the water, she forgot herself and inhaled a big glug of the salty liquid. Her throat filled up, and she started thrashing around, splashing. She yanked herself into the crisp air and coughed and coughed. Her throat burned. She had never been more panicked in her whole life. She felt certain she would drown.

Seconds later, she felt strong arms around her. A swimmer dragged her back toward the boat, and a firm voice commanded, "Grab the handle. Come on. Let's get you back up."

Charlotte did as she was told. With all her strength, she pulled herself back onto the boat and continued coughing. A large hand stretched out across her back.

"Come on. It's okay."

Finally, she forced her eyes open to peer into those same glorious emerald ones.

"Char! Hey! You okay?" Now she heard Lola's voice, down in the water still. She stepped up on the boat's ladder and peered at her cousin anxiously. "What happened?"

"I don't know," Charlotte replied. She coughed again as Jason's hand continued to ease up and down her naked back. "I'm so sorry. I just..."

"What! Don't be sorry," Jason said. "I'm the one who should be sorry. I just tossed you in the water like an idiot. I should have warned you."

"Charlotte's not so good about the water," Lola affirmed.

"Gee. Thanks, Lola," Charlotte said, even though this was 100% true.

"I didn't know." Jason furrowed his brow. "And I won't do that again, okay? Let's just stay up here. I have some not-so-bad vodka in my bag. Want a little bit?"

"Hey! Were you going to hold out on Peter and me?" Lola asked, hands-on-hips and now staring at both of them.

"I just think Charlotte and I deserve it more. We're older, after all," Jason said, laughing.

Charlotte took a little sip and felt her body surge with warmth. Jason wrapped a towel around both of them and huddled close to her.

"The water has always been such a big part of my life," he confessed. "Since my dad works as a fisherman, he took me out fishing for the first time when I was three or four. I remember begging my mom to swim as early as five in the morning once. I could never get enough of it."

"I was always so afraid," Charlotte said. She shook her head, flashing her half-dried hair around her. "My mom never knew what to do with me. But I remember my Aunt Anna used to take pity on me, hold me up, and tell me that if I just kept kicking, she would help me the rest of the way."

"Maybe I can help you lose your fear of the water," Jason suggested.

"Maybe hypnosis would work," Charlotte said with a laugh.

"Ha. We could try that if everything else doesn't work," Jason said.

Charlotte couldn't believe how easy it was to talk to Jason.

The minutes ticked into hours until Peter and Lola begged for Jason to drive them back to the dock so they could go get something to eat. When Lola and Peter dressed and ducked toward the main road, Charlotte and Jason held back and decided to get their food and eat it near the water.

"Suit yourselves," Lola said with a shrug. Her eyes burned into Charlotte's, demanding answers.

Charlotte wouldn't budge.

She and Jason got burgers, fries, and milkshakes and sat on a blanket overlooking the Vineyard Sound. Jason explained a few things about his life that he'd never told anyone before, like how his mother had had such a hard pregnancy and labor with him that she hadn't been able to have any other children. "I think it killed her," he said. "And it's always bothered me that maybe I was never enough for her."

Charlotte's eyes filled with tears. "You? You're obviously enough."

"I don't know," he said, palming the back of his neck.

Charlotte reached over and gripped his other hand. Her fingers laced through his. Her eyes became enormous.

"I've wanted to do this every day since I first saw you," she whispered.

She then bridged the space between them and kissed him. Her heart thudded, and her thoughts raced as his lips opened and accepted her. His hand traced her shoulder and tugged her against him.

When their kiss broke, he whispered, "Why did you wait so long?"

Chapter Two

The Present

Charlotte awoke to a gray and drizzly morning. She stretched her legs until her toes poked up on the other side of the thick comforter. The red numbers on the alarm clock read: 8:42. It was time for coffee, and it was time for another day in this era, which she had decided to call "the rest of her life." Fun.

Standing at the kitchen counter, Charlotte brewed a large pot of coffee and checked her email. Since it was early November, the majority of her current work was for next spring, summer, and early fall—wedding season on Martha's Vineyard. As an event and wedding coordinator, November meant time to think, to breathe.

Since Jason's death, she hadn't been particularly into the whole "time to think" thing. If anything, she needed more to fill her mind with. Dwelling on the past according to grief books she'd read, wasn't doing her any favors, but that's what her brain gave her: images of Jason as that handsome seventeen-year-old; Jason, age twenty-one, getting down on one knee to ask her to marry him; Jason, carrying baby Rachel around the house, rocking her to sleep; Jason—age forty, wearing his finest suit, lying back in the coffin.

No.

Rachel walked into the kitchen area, Charlotte's saving grace from her darker thoughts. She yawned into the words, "Good morning," then reached for a banana in the fruit bowl. "How did you sleep?"

"Not bad," Charlotte lied. In truth, she couldn't remember the last time she had slept like a normal person. "Do you have anything going on today?"

"Just a little bit of homework, I guess," Rachel said. "Oh! And Abby and Gail asked if they could come over. And I kind of said yes."

"What time?"

"Um..."

At that moment, knocks rang out from the front door. Charlotte grumbled and walked through the kitchen toward the foyer. On the route, she spotted no fewer than three photographs of Jason through the years. The photos taunted her, but she couldn't bring herself to take them down. She wanted him there, as much as he could be there.

When Charlotte opened the door that drizzly morning, she found her dear fifteen-year-old nieces, Abby and Gail, along with their mother, Claire, Charlotte's younger sister. Claire lifted a gorgeous bouquet skyward and said, "Do you have any coffee? I'm dying."

"All right. Everyone come in," Charlotte said, heaving a sigh and moving aside to allow them to walk in.

The girls scampered in and hugged Rachel, then collapsed at the kitchen table and began the first of what would surely be a number of hours of gossip. Charlotte leaned forward, hugging Claire.

"They're beautiful. Thank you," she said, taking the bouquet.

"I take it Rachel didn't communicate this little meeting?"

"Not quite," Charlotte said. "But I didn't have plans today, anyway. What do you think? Pancakes?"

"Sounds perfect to me," Claire said. She stretched her legs toward the far end of the kitchen, grabbed a vase from the top shelf, and placed the flowers within. When she turned her gaze back toward Charlotte, she said, "You look like you haven't been eating."

"Gee. Thanks."

Charlotte had a hunch, now, that this whole "getting the girls together" thing was secretly a check-in on Charlotte, the depressed sister. In Charlotte's mind, she had every right to be depressed. One day, her husband had gone out to fish for the morning; the next, she'd had to make preparations to put him in the ground.

Charlotte whipped up a large batch of pancakes. If there was anything she'd had to learn, it was that teenage girls liked to eat. As she stirred in the blueberries, she commented on this to Claire, who laughed.

"Don't you remember? We ate anything that wasn't nailed down," she said.

"I hardly remember that. Once your metabolism dies out, I guess your brain makes you forget about the good times."

Charlotte splayed blueberry pancakes in a big pile on a large red plate. She placed the platter before the three girls and watched as they tore into them, smearing butter and drizzling syrup.

"What the heck. I want one, too," Claire said. "Join me, Charlotte. It's November. Who cares about our thighs till April, right?"

Charlotte laughed and nodded in agreement. In seconds, she had her own thick, doughy, blueberry pancake out in front of her. Rachel poured syrup for her and winked.

"It's best if it's like your pancake went swimming in syrup," she said.

"Great," Charlotte said with an ironic laugh. "Can't wait for the sugar coma."

Abby, Rachel, and Gail seemed secretive about something. They used a code word to refer to someone. "Code Red."

Finally, Charlotte couldn't take it anymore and said, "If you're going to use spy terms around here, you'd better tell Claire and I what you're up to."

Abby grimaced. Finally, she said, "Okay. If you must know, Rachel's in love."

"Come on! Don't just tell my mom that..." Rachel said.

Charlotte and Claire locked eyes—Charlotte could more-or-less remember a similar conversation between herself and Claire a million years ago. Probably, Charlotte had been obsessive about Jason at the time.

"This is so exciting," Claire said, her eyes sparkling. "You have to tell us more. Where did you meet him? What's he like?"

Rachel's cheeks reddened. She glared at Abby. "He's in my history class. But it's not a big deal."

"Everything that's not a big deal is always a huge deal," Charlotte said with a laugh. "Have you talked to him yet?"

"Of course I talk to him, Mom. We're partners," Rachel said. She scrunched her nose up slightly.

"You're braver than me. It took me a million years to work up the courage to talk to your dad," Charlotte said.

At this, Rachel's eyes turned back toward the table. Charlotte immediately regretted it. Bringing up Jason Hamner in just casual, everyday conversations usually soured those conversations in ways you couldn't take back. It was a reminder that nothing had gone the way they had planned, and they couldn't get it all back.

"She's working her magic. That's for sure," Gail said.

"My gosh! What is your magic, Rachel?" Claire asked.

Rachel rolled her eyes and muttered something.

"What did she say?" Claire asked.

"I don't know. Maybe we should just let it go," Charlotte tried.

"No. She said her magic is giving him all the answers on the tests," Abby said with a volatile laugh.

"Rachel! No! Why?" Charlotte demanded.

Rachel gave a half-shrug. "Just because he's the cutest guy I've ever seen doesn't mean he's the smartest."

"Fair enough," Claire said.

"But you shouldn't just give out your answers," Charlotte insisted.

"Come on, Mom. It's just history," Rachel said. "Plus, I think it's unfair that someone can fail a whole class just because they can't remember the exact dates George Washington did something that nobody cares about anymore."

"Hey. We care," Charlotte said.

At this, Charlotte, Claire, and their girls burst into laughter. It was all so ridiculous, so silly.

After they finished their pancakes, Charlotte took the plates and stacked them in the dishwasher. When she turned around, she found Claire's eyes in the doorway.

"What's up?" she asked.

Claire beckoned for her to enter the hallway. When she reached her, Claire said, "What if we try again today?"

Ah. Now Charlotte knew the real reason for the pancake day.

"I don't know," Charlotte said. Her voice was low, almost a whisper.

"Just a few shirts. A few jackets. They're taking up so much of your closet, Charlotte. If anything, I feel like you should buy yourself a whole new wardrobe to fill the space."

"I don't want to fill that space," Charlotte protested. "Those are his things. I can't just throw them out."

"No. You should keep a few key items. Nobody is asking you to throw everything out. But you must see them every single day, right? It's like a weight. You can't escape from it."

Claire turned around quickly and marched down the rest of the hallway toward the bedroom Charlotte had shared with Jason for a number of years before his death. Claire was right, of course: the place looked almost the same as it had before Jason's death. She had even kept Jason's flannel across the desk chair—where he had left it the morning he had gone fishing. When she'd seen it that morning, she remembered specifically thinking, *Oh no. He's going to want that out there. It's a bit chilly today.*

Claire ripped open the wardrobe and splayed her arm out, gesturing toward the thick coats, the jackets, the flannels, and the pairs of jeans.

"The man already had too much stuff," Claire said. She then pointed toward the other side, where Charlotte's trim dresses, tiny pairs of jeans, tank tops, and sweaters took up much less space than Jason's. "I'm just asking you to try to get rid of a quarter of it today. No more. No less."

Charlotte scrunched her nose. "I know you're trying to help," she said. Her voice broke.

Claire's eyes shimmered with tears. "It's not like I would have ever wished this on you, you know."

"Maybe we could try to do this next week? Or the one after? I don't know. It's almost the holidays, Claire. I can't just... forget about him over the holidays."

"Nobody said anything about forgetting," Claire insisted. "But don't you remember what Susan said about going through their mother's things, getting rid of a lot of it, and cleaning up the house? She said it was necessary for them to move on and build something new."

"Anna's been dead since 1993," Charlotte stated. "Almost thirty years!"

"Are you suggesting that thirty years from now—when you're seventy-one years old—you'll be ready to get rid of some of this stuff?" Claire demanded with her hands on her hips.

"Maybe. I think we'd better push it to seventy-five, though," Charlotte said.

"You're being willfully difficult. And I don't know why I'm surprised. This is just what you do," Claire said, trying to joke.

Charlotte perched on the edge of her bed and stared at her shoes. Silence filled the room. Finally, she exhaled and said, "I'll get rid of ten shirts today. Ten. That's it."

Claire snapped her fingers and beamed at her sister. "I'll take it. It's a start."

It was a difficult task, choosing the ten shirts. Claire insisted she didn't have a memory attached to all of them—how could she have? But Charlotte said she did. She could feel all the days she had spent with Jason behind each and every one. She could feel the warmth within the hugs he had given her. By the time she had ten shirts stacked up on the bed, her cheeks were blotchy with tears. When she glanced back at the closet, she winced and said, "It doesn't even look like we did anything."

Claire shrugged. "What's that expression about climbing a mountain? One step at a time?"

"Something like that," Charlotte said.

Claire collected the shirts in her arms and directed herself toward the hallway. "You know, this single guy I know has asked about you a few times."

"What?" Charlotte's stomach curdled at the thought.

"Don't worry about it if you're not ready," Claire said. "I was just thinking; maybe it could be interesting? To go out on a date? Just to see what it felt like to meet someone new?"

Charlotte shook her head violently. She couldn't even articulate how much she didn't want that. Claire heaved a sigh and said, "Very well. I just figured I would at least try. I'll take these to my place and drop them off at a second-hand place in Falmouth when I head off the island next week. Okay?"

She nodded in return. "Okay."

Charlotte was grateful that Claire didn't plan to drop off the shirts at a second-hand place in Oak Bluffs. It would have destroyed her to see one of Jason's friends around town wearing his shirts. It would have felt akin to looking at a ghost.

Chapter Three

Rachel, Abby, and Gail decided to head to the center of Oak Bluffs to meet a few of their classmates, run around in the rain, and probably wind up at one person's house or the other for snacks and movies. As Rachel donned her winter coat and hat, she glanced toward her mother and paused. Her face grew stoic, more like an adult's than a teenager's.

"Are you going to be okay here by yourself today, Mom?" she asked.

"Of course." Charlotte feigned her brightest smile, although she could still hear the faintest quiver in her voice. She was still shaken up about the loss of just ten shirts.

Rachel tilted her head as she looked suspiciously at her mother. "Are you sure? No work to do or anything?"

"You know how it is these days," Charlotte replied. "No weddings till spring. We should appreciate the rest."

"Right. Well. Let me know if you need anything," Rachel said. After another pause, she rushed toward her mother and wrapped her arms around her. She held her for a long moment with her eyes closed.

When Abby and Gail appeared in the foyer, Rachel let Charlotte go. Charlotte's arms ached with the memory of the hug. It took a moment to recover.

"You girls have fun today," Charlotte said, her hand on her hip. "Be safe, and call me if anything goes wrong."

"Right. Like anything ever goes wrong on the Vineyard," Gail said.

You'd be surprised, Charlotte thought.

With Claire gone and the girls off, Charlotte collapsed in a heap near the piano bench and allowed herself to cry for a good five minutes. It was this kind of cleansing cry she started almost every day with, something she had joked with Claire about since she said it also worked as an ab exercise.

When she returned to the kitchen, she scrubbed the sticky table and checked her email again. Her Facebook revealed that Lola had tagged a photo of her from way back in 1996 when she and Lola had palled around together frequently, sometimes with Christine and Claire and sometimes not. In the photo, the girls wore bikinis, and Lola drank one of those bright blue ice drinks. Lola stuck her tongue out to reveal just how blue it was. Charlotte looked sheepish beside her, still in her clothes, and her cheeks bright red from the sun.

Charlotte remembered that summer so well. The summer she had finally kissed Jason—the summer she had officially fallen in love.

Instead of writing anything too dramatic or emotional, Charlotte commented on the photo: **You were obsessed with those blue drinks.**

Lola commented seconds later: **Now, a much different drink does the job for me. Meet up later? PJ's Wine Bar?**

Charlotte considered this. Her schedule for the afternoon

currently involved a lot of crying, remembering, thinking, and crying again, on repeat.

Maybe going out with the girls wasn't such a bad idea.

At that moment, her phone buzzed to reveal a number she didn't recognize. This wasn't such a strange thing, especially given the business she worked in. People referred her all the time to their friends and associates. Well, not *all* the time, but enough to allow her a decent living.

"Hello, this is Charlotte Hamner."

"Charlotte. Hello! It's so wonderful to hear your voice."

Charlotte had zero idea who the man on the other end of the line was.

"Who may I ask is speaking?"

"Oh, I'm sorry. Terribly sorry. I suppose you don't know me. I tend to do that sometimes after I've researched someone so specifically. I feel like I know all about you, but you don't know the first thing about me. Not that you ever have to. My name is Tobias, and I'm the personal assistant for the acclaimed film actress Ursula Pennington. I suppose you must have heard of her."

Charlotte furrowed her brow. Ursula Pennington was one of the more famous twenty-something actresses working in cinema at the moment. She didn't live in a cave, no matter how much she wanted to move there sometimes.

"Of course," Charlotte replied brightly. "Lovely to hear from you, Tobias. How can I help you today?"

"Well, the news is about to hit the stands, blogs, and tabloids. My Ursula just got engaged to the world-famous basketball player, Orion Thompson."

This was a name Charlotte hadn't heard, but she decided to pretend she had.

"Wow. I didn't even know they were dating," she breathed.

"Nobody did! That's what makes it so exciting. It's kind of a last-minute thing, you know, but my Ursula is quite the drama queen. When she gets something in her head, she has to make it happen, you know? That said, when she called me this morning and said she wants to get married on a snow-capped Martha's Vineyard over Thanksgiving weekend, I was like, I don't know how to make that happen! But Ursula said it's this or nothing. So, it has to be this."

Charlotte's jaw dropped. "Thanksgiving is in like, three weeks?"

"It's true. It is. I am staring at a calendar right now as we speak," he continued.

"I've never planned a wedding so quickly," Charlotte confessed.

"Of course. Who would? It's absolutely crazy," he said.

"I just. I mean." Charlotte's thoughts ran in circles. "There's no way to say if it will even snow on Thanksgiving weekend. Sometimes it doesn't. No matter what I do in terms of planning, it's not like I can change the weather."

Tobias seemed at a loss with her.

"I don't know what you want me to tell you," he said. "All I know is this. If you're hired, you'll be working for one of the biggest and most celebrated actresses of her generation. You'll be recorded as the wedding planner for the illustrious Ursula Pennington and her basketball-star husband, Orion. I don't know what you're not getting in this—but you'll be paid handsomely. No. Handsomely isn't the right word. Essentially, the sky's the limit, both on your payment and the cost of the expenses. Imagine a wedding of your wildest dreams, and then double that imagination. Let's create a wedding for Ursula that the world will never forget."

Charlotte was shocked, to say the least. His words felt like bullets to her psyche. She chewed on her bottom lip as she tried to mull over things.

Maybe, if I wasn't so depressed right now, I would go for it.

Tobias, I'm sorry to say—my husband just died in a fishing accident, and I'm not over it enough to handle something as big as this.

Tobias, I actually have decided to put my life on hold for the next thirty years, at which time I'll...

No.

Claire was right.

She couldn't limp around, waiting any longer. She needed to get out of this funk she was in. This was the perfect solution to distract her.

"This will change your life forever, Charlotte Hamner, if you're brave enough to accept the challenge," he said, trying to tempt her.

Charlotte blinked out the kitchen window at the dark clouds that brewed on the horizon. Were they snow clouds?

"I'll go over the numbers," Charlotte said. "I'll assess the possibilities. And I'll have an answer to you—one way or the other—by the end of the day." Then, she cleared her throat and said, "But Tobias. Why me? Why did you contact me for this?"

She had done a number of well-received weddings over the years, including some for celebrities, but nothing of this caliber. Ursula was essentially a goddess among men.

Tobias considered this. "Do you remember those shoes you made for Tiffany Bugman?"

Charlotte furrowed her brow. Tiffany Bugman had been a client the previous summer, several months before Jason's death. When Tiffany had hated the shoes she had purchased for her wedding, Charlotte and Rachel had bought these gorgeous flats and then bejeweled them for Tiffany, adding a bit of flair and pep to a day that Tiffany had said she wanted to be "fun, no matter what."

"Of course," Charlotte replied. "Tiffany was such a great client."

"She's a childhood friend of Ursula's," Tobias said. "Ursula couldn't attend the wedding, as she was filming on location in

South Africa, but she read a long blogpost Tiffany wrote about the event, which spoke at length about the 'specificity and care' undertaken by a particular wedding planner."

Charlotte marveled at this. She hadn't expected that story to return to her like this.

"Goodness."

"Yes, well. Your kindness seems to want to return to you tenfold—in the form of many, many dollar signs. I'll let Ursula know that we're expecting your call." After a pause, he added, "I look forward to meeting you."

With that, the call ended.

Charlotte hovered in the dark shadows of her kitchen as the first snowfall erupted from the dark clouds above. The memory of bejeweling those shoes sizzled through her. She and Rachel had sat at this kitchen table—hard at work for hours at a time. Jason had walked in and out, dotting kisses on their foreheads, hustling back out to fish and returning with snacks for them to eat as they worked. Charlotte and Rachel had complained and grumbled about it, both taking unique pleasure in the shoes' artistry. And when Tiffany Bugman had first seen the shoes, she had burst into tears.

"It's because you care so much about them," Jason had said. "They can see it in your eyes. I get so jealous, you know? I thought you would only care about me for the rest of your life."

Charlotte had giggled at the joke and kissed him. "You're so selfish. You want all my love for yourself."

Chapter Four

Charlotte headed to PJ's Wine Bar later that afternoon, simmering with so much excitement and fear, she thought she might vomit. When she entered the wine bar, Christine and Lola waved their arms manically, then slowly dropped them. Lola's jaw dropped, which left Christine time to say, "You look like you're about to faint."

Charlotte dropped into the spare chair across from them as Christine poured her a hearty glass of merlot. She rubbed her cheeks and then spread her hands to either side.

"Are you going to tell us what's up?" Lola demanded. "Or are we going to have to guess?"

"I'll start," Christine said. "You've fallen in love with a vampire."

"Ha. And he's sucked all her blood," Lola joked alongside her sister.

Charlotte rolled her eyes and tilted her head back to reveal her neck. "No bite marks on me, unfortunately," she said.

"Okay. My guess, next," Lola said. "You've just learned that all this time, Aunt Kerry has been a spy working for the government. She had to make a run for it."

Charlotte giggled. "Mom isn't a spy. At least, I don't think she is. This would explain how she always knew what me and my siblings were up to when we were younger, though."

"See! There's always more to this than meets the eye," Lola said.

Charlotte lifted her glass of merlot and cheered the other two. She then puffed out her cheeks and said, "I think I'm about to agree to the hardest project of my life."

"What?" Lola demanded, her eyes wide with this news.

"Oh my gosh. You're the one who's the spy?" Christine asked. "Spill the details, girl."

"No. I just received a call from Ursula Pennington's personal assistant. Apparently, she's just gotten engaged..."

"To Chris Evans?" Christine asked.

"No," Charlotte said.

"Oh. It must be Bradley Cooper. She was linked up with him for a while," Lola said.

"Neither. Apparently, they've only been seeing one another for a little while, and the whole thing is spontaneous," Charlotte said. "Orion Thompson?"

Christine and Lola turned their eyes toward one another, considering the name.

"A basketball player?" Charlotte said.

"I think Tommy has mentioned him, maybe," Lola said.

"Zach, too," Christine said.

"Well, in any case. The women in our family were never particularly sporty," Charlotte confessed.

Christine pulled up a photograph of the two young lovers, Orion and Ursula, and flashed the image around for all to see. Ursula was a classic blond bombshell, very Marilyn Monroe, with large breasts, large blue eyes, and bright red lipstick.

Beside her in the photograph was Orion himself, who was maybe seven feet tall, towering over her five-foot-four frame.

"They're hot," Lola breathed.

"Yes," Charlotte said. "Looking at them makes me want to faint all over again."

"Have you told them you will do it?" Christine asked.

"Not yet. I said I would say one way or the other by the end of the day," Charlotte affirmed.

"Oh my gosh. Just do it!" Christine said.

Charlotte furrowed her brow. "It's just that, since it's autumn, a lot of the people I would ordinarily hire for something like this have left the island. I don't have the resources I normally have for other weddings. And beyond that, this particular wedding is three weeks away. It's almost impossible."

Lola snapped her fingers. "You should hold it at the Quarry Estate in Edgartown."

Charlotte arched her brow. The Quarry Estate was built in 1888 and was one of the most sought-after wedding venues on the island. Ordinarily, her clients couldn't afford anything like it; it was the lap of luxury, of artistry, teeming with history.

"Let me call them now to see if they have the date free," Lola announced.

Before Charlotte could stop her, Lola was on her phone with the people who owned the Quarry Estate. "November 27. That Saturday. Yes. You have it free?" Lola's eyes bugged out with excitement. "Okay. We need to book it. It's perfect." She then glanced up toward Charlotte and whispered, "And probably Friday as well, right?"

Charlotte's stomach clenched with panic. Was this Lola, pushing her into yet another situation? Before she knew what she had done, she nodded.

"Sure. It has two wings. One side for wedding and reception—the side with that gorgeous view of the water, and the other side for the rehearsal dinner," Christine said, nodding with finality.

"We're going to need it for both nights. That's right," Lola said brightly. "We'll put down the deposit shortly. Thanks so much, Josh. Yep. Talk soon."

When Lola placed her phone back on the table, she clasped her hands together, leaned forward, and said, "Don't think for a minute you're not going to plan this wedding just because a few people left the island for the season. You have me. You have Christine—baker extraordinaire. Your sister does flowers for a living and Zach... He's a world-famous caterer."

Charlotte closed her eyes tightly and rubbed at her temples. In what world could she explain that she just didn't feel up to this? It felt like too much, a weight she couldn't get out from under.

"Oh! And I can write a big description of the event for *The New York Times*," Lola said. "They always like big, socialite parties, especially ones that take place on Martha's Vineyard. It's all a bit sparse now since it's autumn. They'll be hungry for this one. Oh, and since it's so spontaneous—the story will sell for top dollar."

"It's one of the craziest things I've ever heard," Christine affirmed. "Getting married on Martha's Vineyard in three weeks? But we're here for you. We can help with anything."

"And Audrey is so bored at home right now," Lola offered. "Normally, she would complain all day long about doing something like this, but I think she'll jump at the chance to help."

"What about Susan?" Charlotte asked.

"Probably a little too tired yet," Christine said. "The chemo was a success—thank God—but she's still grabbing as much sleep as she can."

"I'm sure she won't refuse if you invite her to the wedding," Lola said.

Charlotte sipped her glass of wine contemplatively. Her

heart hammered with fear. "What kind of cake would you make, Christine?" she asked. "The personal assistant said the sky's the limit in terms of cost. So—the most expensive cake you can dream up. What would it be?"

Christine lit up as she thought for a moment, twirling her glass of wine. "It goes without saying that it should have at least eight tiers on it. Sometimes, I like to go more delicate with the design—like, if it had a number of edible flowers on it, I would find it interesting to make many of the flowers different types. Oh, but I shouldn't get ahead of myself. I only have three weeks to make this thing. I don't want to fall apart, making each unique and individual flower."

Slowly, the pieces began to align themselves in Charlotte's mind. It seemed incredible that anything like this could even come together without a hitch. It was certainly an investment of her time, her energy—and something that had a high probability of killing her or keeping her distracted.

But it was an adventure she couldn't refuse. It was an opportunity of a lifetime.

"Okay. Okay. If you think we can do this..."

"The Sheridan and Montgomery cousins can do anything together," Lola insisted. "I don't want to hear another doubtful phrase from you over the next three weeks."

"Do you think we'll have to skip Thanksgiving?" Charlotte asked.

"No way! We'll just cram the turkey-roasting in with everything else," Lola said.

"I can make pumpkin pie in my sleep," Christine insisted.

"I've seen her do it," Lola affirmed. "It's actually really frightening."

"And you promise it won't break us all up," Charlotte said. The edge of her mouth flickered into a smile.

"No way. We've been through so much worse—and if we

fail this wedding, well... I'm sure it's not the kind of marriage that will last, anyway," Lola said, giving her a wink.

"No way. I'll give them six months regardless of what happens," Christine said.

Charlotte full-on laughed. "Rachel is going to kill me. I just told her we wouldn't have much work for a while. And now, here I am, stuffing us with more work than we know what to do with."

Christine poured them another glass of wine. Outside, snow began to fall, flickering then piling up at the bottom of the windowpane. Charlotte's mind whizzed with images of the now-fast-approaching event. Just before Christine poured that third glass, she lifted her phone and dialed Tobias back.

After one ring, she heard his voice filter through. "Charlotte! It's only been a few hours. Have you made your decision?"

"I have, Tobias. The answer is yes. I'll be in touch shortly with more details. Let's get this world-famous celebrity wed."

Chapter Five

The day before Thanksgiving, Everett sat in limbo in the center of LAX. He had his boots up on his carry-on suitcase; his dark hair was a curly, wild mess; his beard was longer than usual, and his thumb was scanning through the weather report for Martha's Vineyard for the next few days with vague interest.

Snow. It was going to snow.

And the temperature planned to drop down to single digits. *Great.*

Everett shoved his phone into his pocket and blinked toward the flight screen. His plane to Boston was delayed by thirty minutes, then another twenty, and he ached with resentment, mostly toward himself for agreeing to the task at-hand.

"Sure. I'll take photographs of Ursula Pennington's wedding. Whatever. I don't have anything planned." This was what he had said to the editor of *Wedding Today*, one of the ritziest and most sought-after wedding magazines of the era. Photographing big events—like the Oscars, music festivals, and fancy weddings, was something of his bread and butter. In previous weeks, he had been stationed in LA, hopping from one event to another and sending his photographs for payment.

It had been a fine life. The drinks had flowed; beautiful people had turned to him from every direction, hungry for attention in the form of a flashing camera; and he'd had a killer apartment in Silver Lake that friends had told him was a "steal."

Still, it had felt so empty, exacerbated by the fact that Everett was in a pretty heavy fight with his mother and brother, who both lived up in Seattle. He dragged out his phone and again read the most recent text from his mother.

> Your father wouldn't have wanted you so far from home on Thanksgiving.

Great. So, she wanted to play the guilt card, too. That was rich, especially after what she had said. See, Jeff, his brother, was every bit the son his father and mother had planned for. Like their father before him, he was an engineer; he had three children; he'd stayed in Seattle, close to family. Everett had never married; he'd hardly even come close to it. He had allowed his photography career to take him all over the world. He'd had some incredible experiences, and he had met the rich and the famous.

But his mother had insinuated that he didn't have his life together and that he "wasn't really happy."

The happiness part was the worst of it. After all, in Everett's mind, was anyone ever happy? Why did she have to point that out, as a sort of, "I told you so?" It just didn't seem fair.

If he apparently brought such darkness to the Thanksgiving table, then he would just avoid it altogether.

"Thank you, Ursula Pennington," he said.

The outlandishly pricey wedding between Ursula Pennington and one of the best basketball players, Orion

Thompson, had been announced only two weeks prior. The fact that it was to be held on Martha's Vineyard at the end of November was the strangest bit of all. People had questions—and Everett? He had a high price for the photos he planned to take.

The woman he'd kind of dated in Los Angeles the previous month or so had been slightly annoyed at the prospect of his departure. "Why don't you take me with you?" she had asked. "I work in PR. It would be good for me to see what this is like, especially if it turns into the disaster everyone thinks it will be."

"I might be back after. I don't know," he had told her, hating that he couldn't commit to yet another woman, to yet another city.

What was wrong with him? Why was he so different than his family? Why couldn't he find solid ground?

Finally, it was boarding time. Everett stood and waded through the staggering line until he found his seat toward the back of the plane. He stuffed his carry-on in the upper compartment, then leaned back and glanced out the window. The California sun beamed down, never fading.

Now, he was headed toward the snow.

As he waited for the plane to crank up and fly out across the country, Everett thought again of Ursula and Orion, these celebrity millionaires who probably hadn't sat in the likes of Economy Class in a number of years. He imagined that, for them, deciding to marry one another had been a bit more like, "Well, you're rich, and I'm rich. Let's join our rich celebrity forces together, eat caviar, and drink champagne for the rest of our days? Or at least as long as it takes for us to get bored with one another and marry the next hot celebrity who comes along."

When you didn't have problems, Everett knew that you had to create problems out of thin air.

Up in the air, Everett grabbed his camera from its bag and

swiped through a number of the photos he had taken at the celebrity birthday party he'd attended three days before. There were some good shots in there, ones that the "people" would pay to see. He marked the ones he wanted to edit, trashed the bad ones, and then stopped short at the one near the back. For this one, he had apparently been a little drunk and snapped a photo of himself in the mirror of the mansion in Beverly Hills.

The man in the photo was now forty-four years old.

He was handsome, sure—he had always been, with that dark black inky hair, beard, broad shoulders, and cobalt blue eyes. But he looked sadder than he remembered himself looking before, as though when he looked at himself in the mirror, he revealed the inner darkness of his soul.

As the plane hovered over the top of Kansas, he shivered.

Maybe he should have returned to Seattle and made peace with his mother and brother.

Maybe he should have kicked a football around with his nephews, helped his mom bake a pie, and exchanged stories of his father with his brother.

Maybe he had made a huge mistake.

But no. He was already halfway to Boston. Martha's Vineyard—and all that snow—awaited him. He couldn't look back now.

Chapter Six

The day before Thanksgiving, Charlotte sat in a heap in the back of Claire's flower shop. Claire sat across from her; Abby, Gail, and Rachel sat frozen in fear on either side. Before them was a mountain of flowers: roses, lily of the valley, hydrangeas, calla lilies, ranunculus—the list went on and on. The goal of the afternoon was to assimilate them together into several mock-ups for the final bouquet, which they would then decide upon together.

"And if Ursula hates them?" Claire asked breathlessly.

"Then I guess we'll be back on the chopping block," Charlotte said. "But she sent all these examples. She explained that this is her style. We just have to match them and then add a bit of flair to make them, you know."

"Unique," Claire interjected.

"Exactly." Charlotte beamed at her sister.

"So simple," Claire said. She rubbed her eyes, clearly exhausted. Charlotte couldn't blame her. They had been hard at work—back-breaking work—for the previous three weeks. Now, with only three days left until the wedding, it felt like they were at the tail-end of a marathon. Charlotte had made this comparison exactly once, to which Claire had said, "Yeah, as if you would ever run a marathon." Naturally, this hadn't helped.

Claire began to pair up various flowers, her brow furrowed. Charlotte shot up and headed toward her massive book of plans, in which she'd jotted necessary things to remember, phone numbers, people to call, and the timeline of events. She also had it all in her phone, but she tended to like to have things physically in front of her. Rachel teased her for this.

"When does the bride get here again?" Claire called.

"Just after three on Friday," Charlotte said.

"And when is Christine making the pies?"

Charlotte thought for a moment. "I think that's happening now."

"Maybe if you had asked me a few weeks ago, I would have told you that I would have stayed away from the pies for the sake of the dress I'm wearing to this big event," Claire said. "Not now. No way. Let me stress eat some pumpkin pie all day tomorrow, because we need a break."

Charlotte was grateful they had plotted and schemed so hard that they'd allowed themselves Thanksgiving Day off. She needed a day to sit with her mother over a glass of wine. She needed a day to spend with her older sister, Kelli, with whom she had never felt quite as close. She wanted to laugh with her brother, Steven, the oldest one of all, along with his beautiful wife, Laura, and their two children, who were no longer children—Jonathon and Isabella. Naturally, when the Montgomery family got together, there was always that aching hole where Andrew was meant to be.

But Andrew had long-since told them he wasn't coming back. Charlotte knew better than not to take people at their word.

The Sheridan sisters came back. Why not Andrew, too?

Those were thoughts she had to shove into the back part of her mind.

"The second we wake up Friday morning, it's going to be go-go-go again," Claire affirmed. "We have to stay focused."

"Ursula is insane," Abby said suddenly. She lifted her phone up and gestured with it. "She's posting all these photos of her and her friends on her bachelorette trip to Sicily."

"Sicily. Wow," Charlotte breathed. "Let me see."

Abby jumped up from her side of the flower collection and passed Charlotte the phone. There she was: this woman Charlotte had met only over the phone, stationed in a bikini in the sun alongside the sea. Her skin was bronzed from the sun, and she was beautiful and thin. She had popped her knee out to one side like a model for the photograph. Around her was a collection of other sinfully beautiful women, maybe her bridesmaids?

"How many bridesmaids did she say she has?" Claire asked, glancing at the photo.

"Only four," Charlotte answered. "Which I was surprised about. I've heard of women like this having upwards of twenty."

"We couldn't handle twenty," Claire said, scoffing. "I would be on the floor crying with twenty."

"You're going to be on the floor crying, regardless. And I'm going to be right there with you," Charlotte said.

"I don't understand. Why does she want to have a snowy wedding on Martha's Vineyard if she has access to— Sicily?" Gail asked.

"What kind of talk is that?" Charlotte said, teasing her. "Isn't the Vineyard good enough for you?"

Suddenly, the door to the flower shop burst open. Snow fluttered in beautifully as Christine rushed inside, tugging her winter hat off her head. She lifted a brown bag and shook it.

"I figured you girls would want some croissants for fuel?"

"More than anything," Rachel affirmed.

Christine grinned and tugged out the croissants, splaying them on a clean plate. "It's really coming down out there. I hope our Ursula is pleased. She'll have a snow-capped wedding, after all."

As the girls snacked on croissants, Christine scanned her phone and talked about the wedding cake. "I swear, that thing is one of the prettier things I've ever made, but it's nearly killed me."

"Welcome to the club. We all deserve a spa weekend after this," Claire said.

Suddenly, Christine stopped short, lifted her head, and gave them a bug-eyed look.

"What? What is that look for?" Charlotte demanded.

Christine turned her phone toward Charlotte to show an article from a tabloid magazine.

Is the Multi-Million Dollar Wedding Between Ursula and Orion Canceled?

"What?" Charlotte demanded. Her heart felt squeezed. "No. No, no..." She read through the article as quickly as she could.

This reporter has been awake all night, monitoring the specific details of Ursula's well-publicized "bachelorette" weekend in Sicily. There are several hints that allude to the fact that Ursula will not go through with the wedding to Orion this weekend.

Will Ursula leave Orion at the altar?

"Wait a minute," Charlotte demanded. She inhaled slowly and returned the phone to Christine. "No. It's just hearsay. All these bloggers and reporters just want to gossip to get more readers. If I don't hear the wedding is off straight from the horse's mouth, then I'm going to keep going."

"Is the horse in this metaphor Ursula herself?" Rachel asked, teasing her with a bright smile.

"Very funny, young lady." Charlotte reached for a croissant

and took a small bite from the buttery crust. She then grabbed her coat and walked into the gorgeous afternoon, turning her eyes toward the sky and feeling the snow as it flickered and melted across her cheeks.

There really was something magical about Martha's Vineyard in the winter. It felt a bit like a secret, one the rest of the world missed out on since most saw Martha's Vineyard only in her summer glory.

Sometimes, on these snowy days, Charlotte found herself imagining Jason heading toward her from the shadows beyond. She always loved him in his winter coat, his beard thick, and his green eyes reflecting the soft light from the snow. He would always wrap her up in his big coat and dot little kisses across her cheek. "That tickles," she always told him as the bristles of his mustache danced across her skin.

What would Jason say about this wedding?

Jason would say what he always had.

That it was frivolous—but sometimes, the frivolous things in life were the things to celebrate all the more. This was a funny stance from a fisherman. His job, as he always said, was "salt of the earth," the kind of thing you only did if you didn't know how to do anything else. Charlotte had always thought it was pretty romantic to have a fisherman husband. Sure—the smell had been a constant battle for her. She had tried every number of lotions and creams and candles to rid herself of the smell. Claire had always insisted that the smell didn't rub off on Charlotte, but Charlotte had never fully believed it.

Now, she probably would have traded her right arm to have that smell around her again.

She was out of her mind.

Rachel appeared beside her in the snow a few minutes later. She imitated her mother and blinked up at the sky.

"You okay?" she asked.

"Yes, honey," Charlotte replied, easing her daughter's anxiety. "Just plodding forward, trying not to fall apart."

"You've really proven yourself over the past few weeks, I think," Rachel said. "Cool under pressure, despite a lot of things not working out. I thought you were going to scream at Zach when he changed the menu, but you kept yourself calm—"

"Well, I mean, I did scream into a pillow later in the afternoon," Charlotte pointed out.

"Zach's changes are going to work perfectly," Rachel affirmed. "He cares about this wedding just as much as all of us."

"How did you get so wise?" Charlotte asked, looking at her daughter with nothing but love.

Rachel shrugged. "I am almost fifteen now, you know. I guess it was finally time."

Charlotte heaved a sigh, one of hundreds per day, it seemed. "You want to head back in? Help Claire with the bouquets?"

"She is on the verge of crying. I swear she is," Rachel said with a laugh.

When they reentered the flower shop, they found Christine wrapping her scarf around her neck again. She tugged her head toward the door and said, "Those pies won't make themselves, I guess, and we have way, way too many people coming over tomorrow to let them wait."

"You're a master," Charlotte said. She hugged Christine tight and toyed with the little fluff ball at the top of her hat. "Don't know what I would have done without you."

"Well, I guess Lola and I were the ones who pushed you into this. So, without us, you might be a lot more relaxed right now," Christine said with an evil laugh.

"Don't remind me," Charlotte said.

"You won't regret it," Christine replied.

"If you say so."

She watched as Christine walked back into the snowy afternoon. At that moment, Claire hollered and lifted a hand, which she had accidentally clipped with the shears. Bright red blood oozed down her palm.

"No!" Charlotte cried. She rushed toward the bathroom, where she collected a number of bandages and returned to Claire, forcing her to sit.

Claire matched Charlotte's sigh as Charlotte began to bandage her up. It had looked much worse at first; really, it was just a little slash against tender skin.

"The real drama is happening here," Claire said with a half-chuckle. "Not over in Sicily."

"The tabloids should really feature us," Charlotte said as she snapped a final bandage into place.

"The Sheridan and Montgomery sisters lose their ever-loving minds over the wedding of the century," Claire announced, waving her bandaged hand in the air.

"And they all lived happily ever after," Charlotte said with a smile.

"In the insane asylum," Claire finished.

Chapter Seven

Everett rented a car upon his arrival to Boston and drove over to Woods Hole. All the while, snow splattered itself across the windshield, and he forced the wipers to do overtime. He wasn't used to driving in the winter. He had probably done it only a handful of times.

When he reached the ferry service that went between Woods Hole and Martha's Vineyard, the company told him that the only ferries in operation the rest of the night were ones that couldn't support vehicles. He cursed himself for having rented the car at all. He passed his keys over to the valet and watched as the energetic twenty-something eased it down the road and toward another garage. He rubbed his arms and shivered in his light jacket.

"You're not from around here, are you?" the older man who operated the ticket stand asked him.

"I'm not, no," he replied.

"I imagine you're here for this fancy wedding they've got running over there," the man said. "Although I don't want to presume anything."

Everett chuckled inwardly. "You have me pegged."

"I figured. You look like a California man to me," the man said. He swiped a gloved hand across his big, blond beard and beamed at Everett. "You have people you're meeting for Thanksgiving?"

"No. But I'm not much of a traditions guy," Everett said. Even as he spoke the words, he thought, *What does that mean? I love traditions. Why did I just say that?*

"I guess that's fair," the man responded. At this point, Everett could sense that he struggled to maintain that smile. "And you'll avoid that big sugar rush, I suppose." He tapped his stomach and continued. "I myself have a mind to eat upwards of three slices of pie."

Everett suddenly ached to dig into one of his mother's classic apple pies. He could see her now: folding the dough over the cinnamon apples and humming to the radio.

"Here she comes," the man said, gesturing out across the Sound as the ferry boat approached. He stepped away, almost hurriedly, as though any additional time spent with the likes of Everett might erode his soul.

Everett hustled into the belly of the ferry and ordered a hot cup of coffee on board. The coffee tasted burnt, but it warmed up his insides as he sat on the edge of the ferry's indoor portion and blinked out across the waves. On instinct, he checked Instagram and found a photo of two of his closest friends out in Los Angeles, sipping cocktails beneath the sun.

Well, I'm an idiot.

When the ferry reached Oak Bluffs, Everett kicked his boots across the dock and checked his phone again for a taxi service or a rental car company. Against all odds, the wind kicked up even more, whistling past his ears. The chill felt like needles across his skin.

Just down the road, a bright red sign advertised what looked like a hole-in-the-wall bar. He shot toward it and dove through the doorway like his life depended on it. As he blinked into the warm partial darkness, a radio fizzled above, playing a Christmas song. Normally, he grumbled that Christmas songs shouldn't be played till after Thanksgiving. In this case, so far from home—and frozen to the bone—he thought, *I'll allow it.*

Actually, it sounded pretty nice.

He ordered a whiskey from the bartender and sat at a stool toward the far end of the bar, where an antique pinup poster had a Santa hat taped over it, directly over the head. A television in the corner of the room played college basketball on low volume, and several people perched around it, gripping beers and talking in low tones.

The bartender pushed a glass of whiskey in front of him and told him he could pay later. Everett thanked him and shivered again, giving himself away.

"You really have to get a better coat," the bartender said, tapping the side of his nose. "I don't know if you'll make it long in this world if you don't. I'm not much for picking up frozen westerners off the side of the road, but I'll do it if I have to."

Everett gave him a dry laugh. Everyone really seemed to know he was from out west. He wondered if it was something about his clothes? His skin? He had a pretty stereotypical California glow. That must have been it.

At that moment, two women ambled into the bar, yanking off their hats and gloves and marching up to the bartender. They looked similar yet different: clearly sisters, both with glorious brunette hair that draped down their backs and beautiful features. One of them was quicker with a smile than the other, at least here with the bartender. The one that smiled said, "Hey there, Mike. Happy Thanksgiving!"

"If it isn't the Sheridan sisters," Mike, the bartender, greeted them. "You're looking like snow bunnies."

"Just trying to beat the cold. You think we could get two hot toddies?" the smiling Sheridan sister asked. "Christine and I are frozen and looking to drink away our sorrows."

"If you've got sorrows, you know you've come to the right place," Mike said.

Everett shifted on his stool, cursing himself for not ordering a hot toddy. It was perfect weather for it.

The Sheridan sisters sat just two stools away from Everett. The smiling one flipped her hair out and thrust her coat from her long limbs. The coat was too big for her, probably something that belonged to a boyfriend or a husband or something. The fact that it dwarfed her so much made it all the more adorable, Everett thought.

"Tommy keeps making me take this stupid coat out," the woman said. "He says all my coats are for city slickers."

Christine chuckled. "You really made a sucker out of that guy, didn't you? All these years, he's been alone, looking out for himself and himself alone, and now..."

"Ha. I know. He's such a sweetie, too. He said he loved me in his sleep last night," the other woman said.

"Lola!"

Ah! So the smiling one was named Lola.

"I know. It's a little ridiculous." Lola sipped her hot toddy and hollered, "One of your best ever, Mike!" Then, she turned back to Christine and said, "Do you think Charlotte is going to lose it?"

"I think she already has. We're just in the eye of the storm," Christine offered.

"Do you regret telling her to do it? I don't, really. I mean, it's all chaos, and it's been fascinating to watch. But I have to admit that I thought it would pull her out of her depression and in reality..."

"I know." The one named Christine looked as though she pondered this for a moment.

43

"And the fact that Zach changed the menu like that, so soon before the wedding itself," Lola interjected.

Christine's face darkened. "Don't bring Zach into this. He has been killing himself for that menu."

"Yeah, but that decision alone was enough to make Charlotte cry for a full two hours. She had to call Ursula and explain that Zach is this world-renowned chef or whatever and that he knows what he's doing."

"Well, he does know what he's doing," Christine blared. "In case you haven't read some of the reviews that have been written about the Bistro..."

Tensions rose between the Sheridan sisters. Everett swallowed another gulp of his whiskey. It was up to him to take their attention elsewhere. After all, they were somehow involved with this stupid wedding, as was he. It wasn't worth fighting over.

"You said something about Ursula?" he interrupted. "Ursula Pennington?"

Lola and Christine turned their heads toward him. Christine glowered while Lola flashed that all-out perfect smile toward him.

"Yes! The very same. Are you here for the wedding?" Lola asked.

"I am," Everett said.

Christine arched her brow. She seemed not to trust the fact that he had interrupted their conversation like this. "What are you? A groomsman?"

"No. No way. Nothing like that. I guess most of them will fly in on private jets," Everett said with a laugh.

"Sure," Christine said, still a tiny bit annoyed.

"Don't listen to her. We've had a hell of a time getting this wedding together. It was announced last minute, as you probably know, and our cousin Charlotte is the wedding planner," Lola explained.

"That is quite a gig," Everett said, impressed.

"True. We're all helping out as much as we can. Most of our family is on the island, and she has no qualms about ordering us around," Lola said.

"That's good. I'm here to take photographs, mostly for *Wedding Today*," Everett said.

"Oh my God! Charlotte was just featured in that magazine," Christine said. "Someone interviewed her about how frantic it's been, planning a wedding for a celebrity in just a few weeks. I read the article. It was great."

"I guess this is the kind of wedding that changes the wedding industry," Everett agreed.

"You don't seem particularly enamored with the idea of weddings," Lola said with a smile.

"I wouldn't call myself that, no. But they can be beautiful when done right."

"We've never been married, either," Lola said.

"Not yet," Christine said.

"There's always time," Everett said. "At least, that's what I always tell myself. I hope I'm right."

They continued to talk: about Everett's career as a photographer and about the places he had gone to work. He and Christine realized that they'd been at the same event a few years before in Paris when Christine had entered her cake into a pastry chef competition.

"Some of those cakes were absolutely extraordinary," he told her. "I thought I was going to lose my mind, not being able to eat them."

"I feel the same way when I make them," Christine returned. She seemed a bit looser, a bit friendlier. Maybe she regretted how she'd been when they had initially met.

Lola ordered another round of drinks and insisted it was on her. She then lifted her arms skyward, popping her shoulders. "I realized we never got your name," she said.

"Oh. I'm Everett. Everett Rainey," he said. He dropped his hand out, and she shook it, maintaining that pretty smile.

"I'm Lola. This is Christine." She arched her brow, then pretended to hunt around the bar for a moment. "I guess you're here by yourself. Nobody to celebrate Thanksgiving with?"

"Afraid not," Everett said. He tried to make sure his grin didn't waver; he wasn't sure he was successful.

"You should celebrate with us!" Lola suggested.

Christine gave her a look like, *I can't believe you just said that.*

But even she echoed it next. "Yeah. Why not? We already have a million people eating with us. Why not a million and one?"

"Are you sure I'm not putting you out?" Everett asked, looking at one and then the other.

"Not at all," Lola insisted. "Plus, you can meet the wedding planner herself. She's a true genius, although she would never admit that."

"I can't resist meeting a genius," Everett replied with a large grin.

"Plus, you can't insult Christine and miss out on all the pies she's been baking all day long," Lola continued.

"I'm up to my ears in pies." Christine nodded.

"What kinds?"

"Pumpkin. Pecan. Apple," Christine said.

"Apple's my favorite," he said.

"Then I have a bone to pick with you," Christine said, giving him a mischievous smile. "Because they're the hardest to make. All that chopping!"

Everett thought again of his mother, up to her elbows in apple peels. Why hadn't he ever offered to help?

"Where are you staying tonight?" Lola asked.

"Over in Edgartown," Everett said. "I just have to figure out how to get over there."

"No, no. You're not going that way," Lola said. "The roads are way too bad after all this snow, and my family owns an inn just a few blocks away. You're coming with us."

Everett laughed. "It's really not a problem. I can call a taxi."

"Nobody on this island wants to drive your sorry butt across it so late at night before Thanksgiving," Christine retorted.

Everett turned toward Mike, who heaved a sigh and said, "I would think twice before you argue with the Sheridan sisters. If they get the other one over here to finish the job, you really don't have a chance."

"There's another of you?" Everett asked, arching an eyebrow.

"Susan. And she's the harshest one of all," Lola affirmed.

About an hour later, Lola and Christine led Everett through the snowy center of town, back toward the docks, and then on down toward the Sunrise Cove Inn, which they said had been in their family for generations. The place was picturesque in every way, with big windows that captured views toward the water, a cozy foyer interior with a big antique desk, and an attached bistro, where Christine apparently worked as the pastry chef.

The front desk was empty, and Lola had to rush to the side to flick on the lights. "Shoot. I guess nobody is staying here at the moment. Did Susan say anything about that?" she asked Christine.

"She mentioned that there will be a few people checking in on Friday," Christine said. "But, I would check the schedule to see which rooms are available."

"You're probably staying all weekend, right?" Lola called as she snuck back toward the office.

"Guess so," Everett said. He scanned the little foyer until his eyes found a hanging portrait of a family: a woman who very much seemed the spitting image of both Christine and

47

Lola, with her arms wrapped around three darling girls. A man towered over all of them, the formidable father.

It was funny, Everett thought, the types of people you met on the road. He could never fully prepare himself for it.

"Here we go," Lola said brightly, directing him toward a staircase that wound up toward the higher floors. "Your room is on the third floor. It has a beautiful view of the Sound. I think you're going to love it."

Everett followed her up and paused outside the room as she turned on the lights and inspected it. "Looks clean to me," she said. "What do you think?"

"It's perfect. All I need is a place to lay my head," he said.

"Ha. You're so charming," Lola responded. "Don't make the bride run away with you."

He laughed as Lola walked around him, back toward the hallway. "We have Thanksgiving dinner at around one in the afternoon." She reached into her purse, grabbed a little piece of paper, and scribbled the address. She then passed it to him. "Does that work for you?"

"Of course. Should I bring anything?"

"Don't be silly. We'll have more than enough of everything to go around. Just prepare yourself mentally for my family. We can be... a lot."

Everett—whose family had always been bitter, cross, quiet —grinned wider. "I think I can handle it."

Chapter Eight

I t was one in the morning on Thanksgiving Day. Charlotte hovered over the dining room table at the Sheridan family house, her phone pressed hard against her ear, as she strained to hear Ursula's personal assistant, Tobias, from all the way in Sicily. In front of her was her massive book of dates, times, and details, along with a filled glass of wine, a half-eaten croissant, and Audrey and Rachel, in two different chairs, both on the verge of falling asleep.

"What was that, Tobias?" Charlotte asked.

"I said that the snow you guys have been getting—wow! It's um. It's a lot. I spoke with our private pilot, and he's a bit nervous about the weather," Tobias said.

Charlotte furrowed her brow. *It was you guys who talked non-stop about this snow-capped wedding or whatever. The weather is here, and you're not ready for it? What's that about?*

"We're still receiving most of our flight traffic," Charlotte replied. She had spoken at length with one of the airport operators that afternoon. "I don't think you'll have trouble landing.

It's Martha's Vineyard. We're used to handling a good bit of snow."

Tobias lowered his voice ominously. "I think our bride has grown a tiny bit anxious about the whole affair and is looking for any reason to rip me in two, to be quite honest with you, Charlotte."

"I see."

"But I'll speak to her. I'll assure her again that the flights won't be a problem." He paused for a moment.

In the background, Charlotte could hear a flurry of spoken Italian. "You must be homesick, so far away on Thanksgiving," she said.

"Oh, not at all," Tobias said. "I love this life. I get to go all over the world. And really, Ursula is a dear friend. It's just a chaotic week for all of us. I look forward to sending her off on her honeymoon, so I can sit down with a piece of pumpkin pie and shut my own pie hole for a little while." He chuckled, then added, "Thank you for your patience, Charlotte. You've been a dream. And I know the wedding will go off without a hitch. Or —if there are any hitches—I know you'll find a way to iron them out."

"That's what I do," Charlotte said.

When Charlotte hung up, she sent along another brief of information regarding where the bride was meant to stay in the mansion, where the groom was meant to stay, where their family members would be stationed, and where the bridal party was meant to go. Of course, Charlotte would be there with them every step of the way to ensure there weren't any mishaps. In her experience, however, it was always better to send the info ahead of time, just to keep things organized.

What would I do without you?" Jason had always said, referring to her organizational skills.

Admittedly, if Charlotte had allowed Jason to handle things like yearly taxes, he would have somehow found a way to foreclose the house and maybe even get them arrested. He was that bad.

Audrey hiccupped awake and blinked at her mother's cousin. She placed a hand over her pregnant stomach and said, "Is everything okay? You sounded... stressed."

"Have I gone a single moment without sounding stressed since this all began?" Charlotte asked.

"Good question. The answer is no," Audrey said, delivering that sneaky smile of hers.

"What are you guys doing still up?" Susan Sheridan walked down from the top floor of the Sheridan residence, wigless, her hair still incredibly short after all the chemo. She gave them a sleepy smile and turned her attention to the book on the table before Charlotte.

"Just last-minute wedding things," Audrey said. "And I'm working hard."

"Or hardly working," Charlotte said, teasing her.

"It's horrible, the things places of employment make pregnant people do these days," Audrey affirmed.

That moment, the back door opened to reveal Christine and Lola, talking a bit too loudly, revealing their tipsiness. When they arrived to the kitchen, Susan pressed her finger over her lips and said, "Shush! Dad's asleep."

"Oops," Christine said, before bursting into giggles.

"What's gotten into you guys? Where were you?" Susan asked.

Charlotte rolled her eyes inwardly. Although her cousins had been incredibly helpful over the past few weeks, she couldn't help but ache with jealousy at their ability to just go out and get drunk.

"It's the night before Thanksgiving, Susie!" Lola said. "And we met a handsome stranger at the bar. He's a photographer. We wanted to flirt, of course, but we were good girls."

"I see," Susan said. She turned toward the freezer, yanked

out a large bag, then proceeded to slice at Christine's home-made cookie dough, which they liked to keep on hand for just these occasions.

"Fantastic idea!" Lola said. She then walked toward Audrey and ruffled her hair. "How's my little pregnant mouse?"

"I'm more like a frog these days. Or a pig, better yet," Audrey groaned.

"Anyway, it looks like this photographer is going to join us for Thanksgiving dinner," Christine said. She drew off her coat, then disappeared to hang it up. "He has a lot of interest in Charlotte's work as a wedding planner. He's a photographer for *Wedding Today!*"

This piqued Charlotte's interest for the first time. She yanked her head around and said, "Did he say which weddings he's photographed before?"

"I don't think so. But he's not really the type of person to brag about that stuff," Christine said. "We did discover we've crossed paths a few times. Both of us single through our thirties, working on our careers—that kind of thing."

"So, he's not married?" Susan asked, arching a delicate eyebrow.

"Susan always wants everyone to be married," Lola said.

"I don't think that's such a bad thing," Susan replied. "So what? I want everyone to have the kind of happiness I used to have with Richard that I now have with Scott."

"Then what's keeping you kids from getting hitched?" Audrey asked.

Susan rolled her eyes as she settled each cookie dough slice on the baking sheet.

"Aunt Charlotte," Audrey breathed. "Hey. Aunt Charlotte..."

Charlotte did generally like that Audrey called her Aunt.

They were all one big, happy, weird family, after all. But her mind was abuzz with wedding info, and she barely blinked up.

"I just want a piece of cookie dough, pre-baked. Well, pregnant baby wants it," Audrey said.

Charlotte heaved a sigh, turned around, and collected a slice of the frozen cookie dough into her hand. After her delivery, she turned back and retrieved a morsel for herself. After that, everyone else chimed in with similar needs.

By the time the cookies were baked and the first round eaten up, it was nearly two in the morning. Charlotte had finalized even more details about Friday and Saturday and had managed to cook up even more anxiety than she'd had before.

"I think we should call it for the night," Susan said.

Christine and Audrey had collapsed on the couch. Rachel sat on the floor with Christine's cat, Felix, and rubbed his neck. Lola nibbled at another cookie while scanning her Instagram feed.

"We have so much to do tomorrow. So much to prepare for!" Susan said.

Charlotte grinned inwardly. She snapped at the end of her pen and gave a little shrug. "I guess that's all I can do for the day, huh?"

"And you promised you'll take all day tomorrow off, right?" Susan said.

"It'll be a challenge," Charlotte said, wiping her hands on a towel.

"We'll all watch you like a hawk and make sure you're living in the moment. No matter what," Lola said with a funny smile.

Charlotte watched as everyone slowly walked toward their separate bedrooms. Scott, Susan's high school boyfriend and now, again, boyfriend, had built onto the house, allowing for two extra big beds in two bedrooms.

Still, even though they were frequently invited to stay, Charlotte never felt comfortable waking up in a house that wasn't the one she, Rachel, and Jason had lived in together. It wasn't anything she'd ever been able to explain. It was simply necessary, always, to her that they go home.

Plus, it was only a twenty-minute walk away.

Charlotte and Rachel bundled themselves up and hugged Susan goodbye. Susan insisted they come over as early as possible, both to help and gossip with the rest of the girls. "Amanda and Jake will be here around noon, I think, along with my grandbabies and their mama," she said, squeezing Charlotte's elbow with excitement. "I just can't wait."

Charlotte and Rachel walked through the snow back toward their home. They both wore thick snow boots and stuffed their hands into their pockets. Charlotte studied the way the moon reflected against the snow, as beautiful as any painting.

"Mom?" Rachel asked suddenly as they made their way across the center of Oak Bluffs.

"What is it?"

"I can't wait for this wedding to be over," Rachel admitted.

Charlotte laughed. Her laugh echoed from building to building and then swept out across the water, through that impossible darkness that lurked between this island and the mainland. She wrapped an arm around Rachel's shoulder and squeezed her tightly against her.

"I know, baby. I feel the same way."

But did she? Charlotte had ached to think about anything else but the sadness in her heart. And as she clicked the key into the lock and shot open the door of their now two-person home, she marveled that she was perhaps further from heartache than she had been in the past year.

Business was an antidote, or maybe, it was just something to hide behind.

"Happy Thanksgiving, Rachel," she breathed, watching as her daughter swept toward her bedroom. "I love you, and I'll see you in the morning."

"Happy Thanksgiving. Love you too, Mom."

Chapter Nine

Everett awoke on Thanksgiving morning just after eight-thirty, which was a California man's five-thirty. He rubbed his eyes and guffawed at the enormous amount of snow outside his window. It had shaken itself out over the boats that were latched to the docks, stacked itself over the nearby parked cars, and made itself up like icing on the tip-tops of trees.

It would be a winter wonderland wedding, after all.

Everett had placed the note Lola had given him on the bedside table. He lifted it to read the address again. A quick check on his phone revealed that wherever this was, it was just down the road. It marveled him to imagine it: a life of growing up on Martha's Vineyard, walking to your job at the Sunrise Cove Inn, spending long days on boats, and sunning beneath that glorious New England sky.

He was probably just romantic about it because he had never been to Martha's Vineyard. He'd been all over the world but never here. He always got misty-eyed over places he didn't understand.

Everett stood in front of the mirror shirtless and analyzed himself. After living a number of months in LA, he hadn't done much in terms of "eating badly" and had certainly chiseled his abs down to an impressive six-pack. He dropped to the carpet and did one hundred crunches, then turned over to do one hundred pushups. All the while, he told himself to call his mom, just to check in. Not now—not at six in the morning west coast time. He would call later just to let her know he cared and to wish his family a Happy Thanksgiving.

When he got up from the floor, he snapped on the TV to watch the start of the Macy's Day Parade. He had fond memories of watching this, nibbling on a Thanksgiving treat, his brother beside him. He wondered if his brother's children liked the Macy's Day Parade as much as they had. But what was it, exactly, that they had liked? The floats? The dancing? The idea of other people eating parade candy?

He had no idea.

But he did waste a lot of that morning watching it. After that, he headed over to the Sheridan house, dressed in a dark blue button-up shirt, one he knew brought out his eyes, a pair of dark blue jeans, and his boots. On his walk, the sun warmed his back, a welcome thing after the previous night's chill.

When he reached the Sheridan house, he was overwhelmed by the number of cars in the driveway. Christine and Lola had said there would be a number of guests, that he would be the one million and first. He had thought they'd been exaggerating. When he reached what seemed to be the back door, he rapped on the screen door as loud as he could before just barging in. He dropped his boots awkwardly in the mudroom and then continued on toward the kitchen, where he found some fifteen people, either crammed around a table or seated in front of the television or stationed around the kitchen counter. Outside, even more people stood around a picnic table on the porch that overlooked the Sound, warmed with stand-up heaters that were normally used at restaurants.

An older man toward the far end of the room gave him a curious, not-overly-welcoming smile. At that moment, Lola burst down the stairs and stretched her arms wide in greeting. She barreled into him with a hug.

"Everyone! This is Everett. Christine and I met him at the bar last night. Apparently, he's taking some photos at the big wedding. Not the trashy tabloid photos, either," she explained.

Everett had to laugh. It was clear that she had already had a few glasses of wine.

"Happy Thanksgiving, Everett!" A pregnant girl sat near the television with a fist full of M&M's. She waved with her other hand. "I'm Audrey, Lola's daughter she had out of wedlock. As you can see, I'm following suit."

Everett chuckled nervously. Another woman with very short hair approached. Her features were similar to Lola and Christine, although she looked a bit stricken, a bit exhausted.

"I'm Susan, Lola and Christine's other sister," she said. "And you're so welcome. Can I get you a glass of something? We've got the wine flowing."

More and more people went around the room, calling their names and greeting Everett. There was Steven and his wife, Laura, and their children. Then, there was Claire and her daughters, Abby and Gail, along with her husband, Russell. Amanda and Jake were introduced as Susan's children. "Amanda's studying to be a lawyer like her mom," was something the older gentleman toward the side of the room interjected, which led Everett to learn that Wes was Lola, Susan, and Christine's father. Beside him was "Uncle Trevor," the father of Steven, Kelli, Claire, and Charlotte.

"Charlotte's the wedding planner," Lola interjected. "Although we haven't been able to track her down for quite a while..."

"I'm sure she's off somewhere finalizing something else in that silly wedding," Susan said as she poured Everett a glass of wine.

"Mom! Come on. It's not silly," Amanda argued playfully. "It's going to change Aunt Charlotte's career forever."

At that moment, another guy around Amanda's age snuck in from the porch, kissed Amanda on the cheek, and then introduced himself as Amanda's fiancé, Chris.

Everett's heart pounded with each new person. *I didn't know families could really be like this—the way they are in the movies. Everyone is so welcoming. So eager. So loving.*

"Oh, and you absolutely have to taste one of Christine's croissants," Susan said. She dropped into a cupboard to drag out a big basket of buttery, flaky morsels. "I wanted to save them for dinner, but you look like you haven't nibbled on anything yet today, Everett."

"He looks like he eats healthy," Uncle Trevor said. "We don't want any of that around here, Everett. Not on Thanksgiving."

"Hear, hear! The day we celebrate all things sugar and fat!" Audrey called from the corner as she cracked through another few M&M's.

"Where's your family these days, Everett?" Uncle Trevor asked.

"They're up in Seattle," Everett replied. He sipped his wine idly, then added, "My father passed away a few years ago, so it's just my mom and my brother and his family up there."

"You must be sad to miss out on dinner with them," Uncle Trevor said as he leaned up against the counter.

"I really am," Everett said. Again, he was surprised to really feel that sadness. He hadn't expected it and had kind of rushed across the continent, hoping that any of that would remain out west.

"Well, it's a good thing you met our Lola and Christine out at the bar," Trevor said.

At that moment, three men stomped in from the porch, where, it seemed, a grill had been lit. They introduced themselves as Zach, the cook, Tommy, and Scott, who wouldn't let anyone else light the grill.

"You're in for the wedding, right?" Zach asked, sliding past him and back into the kitchen. He yanked open the oven to check on the last of the turkey.

"Yep," Everett said.

"I'm the chef for that thing," Zach said. "I've spent the past few weeks training all these caterers, some of whom I've worked within the past, and others... not so much." He snapped the oven door back into place and then slipped his hands across his apron. "I have this busboy, Ronnie, who works with me at the bistro. Suffice it to say that the kid is an anxious wreck. But he looks at this wedding as another chance to prove himself. I'm a sucker, I guess, and I'm letting it happen. But the first time he drops a tray at this multi-million-dollar wedding..."

Christine snuck up behind Zach and wrapped her arms around his middle. Her eyes connected with Everett's. "Don't mind him. My boyfriend is a little cynical when it comes to all this."

"Not cynical. Just worried," Zach said, rubbing her arms.

"Don't bring all those doubts in here," Lola said. "You'll make a mess out of Charlotte."

"But it's not like anyone has seen Charlotte in the past hour," Audrey insisted.

Susan shot through the group again, grabbed a spare plate, and filled it with various things from the dining room table—appetizers, she called them. She then pointed to a big vat and said, "Aunt Kerry made some of her famous clam chowder. If you don't eat some of it, she'll never forgive you."

Everett poured some clam chowder into a small bowl and

then sat on the floor near Audrey's feet. This motion put him face-to-face with a beautiful orange kitty, who looked at him ominously. Wes bent down to bring the cat into his arms.

"Don't mind him," Christine said. "He's a New Yorker through and through. Still hasn't taken to the whole family dynamic thing."

"Oh, but he loves me," Wes said, singing the words.

"Yeah, yeah. He loves Dad," Christine said, rolling her eyes.

Through all this, Everett was suddenly struck with the realization that the young woman in the portrait in the lobby of the Sunrise Cove Inn—the woman who seemed to be Lola, Christine, and Susan's mother—wasn't among them.

His heart darkened.

Again, he felt the push to call his own mother.

But it was still early on the west coast.

And what could he possibly say?

That moment, another knock rang through the house.

"That's probably Stan," Lola said. She popped up from her chair and stretched her legs toward the back door. Moments later, another older guy followed in after her. She gestured toward him and said, "Everett, this is Stan. Stan, this is Everett. This is Stan's first Thanksgiving with us, isn't it, Stan?"

Stan looked about as nervous as Everett felt. He prayed that his face wasn't so blotchy and that his hands didn't shake. In the awkwardness that fell, Tommy strode forward and placed a hand on Stan's lower back.

"I got a chair all set up for you, Dad," he said. "Just this way."

Dad? They didn't look anything like one another. Everett snapped a pretzel between his teeth and made peace with never really understanding the Sheridan clan at all.

Everyone seemed locked into their own conversations, which left Everett to stir in his mind for a second. He turned his head right so that his eyes peered through the legs of the dining room table and toward the yonder bedrooms. One of the doors was open, just a crack to reveal a lilac-painted bedroom.

He had a hunch that someone was in there.

He could feel someone's voice echoing through the crack.

You had to focus on it to know it was there.

Everett stood, placed his half-eaten appetizer plate on the counter, and snapped his hands together to scrub off the crumbs. When he reached that crack in the door, he bent down, curiosity taking hold of him. Nobody else in the dining area, kitchen, or living room noticed him.

"I understand that, Ursula, I do," a voice said.

The voice was beautiful, fluid, girlish yet sure of itself. Everett would have said it reminded him of a song if he had been the sort of poetic human to do something like that (which he wasn't).

Still, the voice itself captured his curiosity, along with his realization that, in actuality, this woman spoke to Ursula Pennington herself.

"I understand it's been a hard journey," the woman continued. "And that the private plane wasn't as well-stocked as you'd been led to believe. Unfortunately, I wasn't in charge of that portion of your..."

Oh, this poor woman. Everett had dealt with a number of celebrities over the years, but it never seemed to get easier.

"You're still on track to arrive tomorrow afternoon, aren't you?" Charlotte asked. "No, no. I understand that it's essential you eat only fish in the days leading up to... I'm sure you'll look remarkable in your wedding dress. It was how many million dollars? Oh. Yes, that should be enough, then. ... No, it was a joke. Terribly sorry. Yes..."

Everett chuckled to himself. Ursula had trapped her. Now, this woman was in a kind of labyrinthian hellscape for the next two and a half days—maybe a little bit more. He pitied her.

Suddenly, however, the door yanked open, and there she stood: the wedding planner.

And her eyes reflected danger.

She knew he'd been spying on her.

He had been caught.

Chapter Ten

Charlotte still felt vaguely a part of another world. Ursula's voice—now a borderline screech, so close to the wedding—still filled her ears as she stood, her chin lifted, her eyes peering into the most glorious cobalt blue ones. The man in the crack of the door at the Sheridan house was entirely too handsome, his dark brown hair shaggy but in a model-way, and his lips just the slightest bit crooked, as though he was always on the verge of uproarious laughter.

"And what else, what else..." Ursula continued, clucking her tongue over the line. "I swear, there was something else I wanted to go over with you. Gosh, I just cannot..."

"You know what? You can give me a call if you think of it," Charlotte said, witnessing her first opportunity to jump off the line in over forty minutes.

"I would really lose my head if it wasn't for you, Charlotte," Ursula said, erupting into giggles. "Pardon me. My mother's just given me a huge glass of champagne. How am I meant to...?"

With that, Ursula hung up the phone. Apparently, she had lost interest.

Charlotte exhaled, filling her cheeks with air. She dropped her phone against the little wardrobe beside her and furrowed her brow at the stranger.

"Are you a spy sent over from Ursula's team?" she asked.

He laughed. Gosh, his laugh was deep and delicious, really, when compared to Ursula's voice.

"Yes. Ursula Pennington herself sent me all the way to this overly quaint Thanksgiving dinner just to torment you over pie," the man said with a grin.

"I knew it," Charlotte offered. She tilted her head against the doorframe. Although she had only had a half-glass of wine, her brain felt all foggy. "I should have known she wouldn't let me get away with ruining her wedding. I had it all plotted out."

What was she doing, joking about something she cared so deeply about?

"Oh yeah? Tell me more," the man said.

"Well, first, there's the threat of the apocalypse," Charlotte said. "I thought that would go really well with the pre-wedding drinks."

"It's nice to put the fear of God in everyone just as the first cocktails are poured," the man agreed.

"And then, as Ursula walks down the aisle, I thought it would be pretty cool to have a meteorite strike through the roof of the mansion and crash into the altar. Nobody's hurt, of course—"

"Again, just reminded that they're not safe. Not even on Martha's Vineyard," the man continued.

"But the worst of it is that some of the crab cakes at the reception will give you food poisoning, and some of them won't," Charlotte said, bubbling over with laughter now. "So it's kind of like playing Russian Roulette, you know? If you want to eat a crab cake..."

"Then you had better be ready for the consequences," the man said.

It had been years since Charlotte had bantered with a stranger like this. They held one another's gaze for a moment longer until the man turned toward the kitchen counter, grabbed one of Christine's croissants, and passed it toward her —like a peace offering.

"I'm sorry for spying on you," he said. "I promise I won't reveal any of your secrets."

Charlotte laughed and spun back toward the bed. She sat on the edge and swung her feet out in front of her, like a much younger girl.

"Actually, it's this snow. It's what she wanted, you know? But now, the string quintet I hired is having a difficult time getting here, and Ursula is ready to blame me for all of it. I'm like—I don't have control over the weather! No matter how many weddings I've planned or how many post-it notes I've stuck to my office door, I can't demand that God make it snow, but only a specific amount," she said. She then took an overly-large bite of her croissant and studied her toes. One of her socks had a massive hole near the big toe. She hadn't noticed. It wasn't like her not to notice something like that.

"I'm going nuts," she muttered.

The man remained in the doorway, looking at her with that same half-smile.

"You should really give yourself a few hours off," he said suddenly. "Your whole family is out there waiting for you."

"Ha. I don't think any of you understand all the work I still have to do," Charlotte said. "I don't mean it in a negative way. Just that... if I don't stay on top of myself, Ursula herself will bury me six feet under."

"Think of that headline," the man said. "World-famous actress murders wedding planner on Martha's Vineyard."

"It would give the wedding a lot of press, for sure," Charlotte said. "Maybe I should schedule it for after the wedding, before the photography session."

The man seemed to think every single thing she said was gold. After his laughter calmed down, he said, "If wedding planning doesn't go through, maybe you should think about comedy."

"Great. So I can look like a fool in front of even more people?"

"Something like that." He cleared his throat and then added, "I've photographed tons of weddings like this. Big, multi-million dollar, everything-on-the-line weddings, and, even though it always looks like everything is about to crumble just before, I have to assure you: everything always clicks into place. Sometimes, it happens at the last minute. Sometimes, the wedding planner really does end up on the floor in pain. But you seem more organized than those fainting wedding planners."

"Ha. Well, I have already bragged about my post-it notes," Charlotte said. She gripped the stem of her wine glass and sipped it delicately. "You must be the photographer. The one working for *Wedding Today*."

"My reputation precedes me," the man said.

"But not your name. What is it?"

"Everett," the entirely too-handsome man called Everett said.

"Charlotte."

They shared another secret smile. From the other room, Charlotte's father, Trevor, burst into applause and commanded one of the basketball players to "get the ball!"

"I never really understood sports," Charlotte said to Everett. "But that's my dad out there, howling at them like the players can hear him."

"I was always a little too arty for all that," Everett confessed.

Charlotte dropped her head back and sipped the rest of her wine. By the time she opened her eyes again, Everett was there before her with a full bottle of merlot. He poured her a second glass and then filled his own. As there wasn't anywhere else to sit in the bedroom, and the living room and kitchen were blurry with activity, Everett sat at the edge of the bed next to her. Although he was more than six inches away, the heat of his body emanated across her arm.

"So. Yeah. You work for *Wedding Today,*" Charlotte breathed.

"They just interviewed you," Everett said.

"True. Very true. And in the interview, I talked about all this like it's second nature. Since you just eavesdropped on me, you could easily go off and tell them all about my lies. Nothing about this is second nature. I'm just dragging myself through it, making it all up as I go along. And the amount of money I'm responsible for! Do you know how crazy that is? I still buy off-brand cereal!"

"It tastes the same!" Everett retorted, flashing her a smile.

Why was he so endearing?

Charlotte furrowed her brow. "So you won't tell them—about the very real fact that I'm a complete and utter mess."

"Compared to the other wedding planners I've seen, you're basically a queen," Everett said. He then clinked his glass with hers.

From where they sat, they could hear Christine and Zach discussing what was left to prepare for Thanksgiving dinner.

"Christine, can you just keep an eye on those yams."

"Zach, the sauce! You almost knocked it over."

"Christine, where did you put the pies? Ah, there. Wait, how many did you make again?"

"Fifteen. I figured fifteen would be enough?"

Zach laughed uproariously. "With these monsters? They eat everything in sight. Especially that one there."

At this point, Audrey marched past the counter, furrowed her brow at Zach, and said, "Excuse me? Are you talking about a pregnant woman right now?"

Charlotte chuckled. "You probably think my family is insane."

"Maybe a little," Everett said. "Much louder and more alive than my family back in Seattle. It's a different change of pace. I can't say I dislike it."

"Just because you're up to your knees in wedding planning doesn't mean you can talk to me about how many pieces of pie I eat on Thanksgiving, Zachary!" Audrey said, placing a finger on the counter between them.

"I can't tell if she's kidding or not. Are any of them kidding?" Everett asked under his breath.

"It's sometimes difficult to tell when it comes from Audrey," Charlotte said. "She's on the snarky side for sure. But also, Christine and Zach have been huge helps with the wedding—but they're just as stressed as me in different ways. I can't imagine what they feel now, having to feed all of us today."

"You know what, Audrey? You know what?" Suddenly, Zach lifted a can of whipped cream and smeared a line of it across Audrey's nose and upper cheek.

Audrey made a funny screech, grabbed the whipped cream bottle, and spun it around on Zach's face.

"Children!" Christine cried.

"He started it," Audrey said.

Susan rushed in from upstairs, bug-eyed, then burst into laughter at the sight of both Audrey and Zach, their faces white with whipping cream.

"You've got to be kidding me," she said, wiping tears from her eyes. "You know we have a guest here with us today. You can't just act like idiots."

"Who's our guest again?" Audrey demanded. She turned

her face back toward the bedroom where Everett and Charlotte sat, sipping wine. "Is it that guy who's already hitting on Aunt Charlotte?"

"Oh my gosh, Audrey," Lola said from the far end of the room. "Give it a rest."

"Yep. Your family definitely has more personality than mine," Everett said, taking this awkwardness as an excuse to get up from the bed.

Charlotte felt vaguely cold and alone as he walked back toward the doorway. When he turned back, she had the funniest idea to tell him to stay. As though he mattered.

"Sorry I interrupted your work," he said. He pretended to tip a fake hat.

"Don't worry about her," Lola said, forcing Everett's head back around. "She's just grumpy because she wants to eat. How much longer, Christy?"

"You know I hate when you call me that," Christine barked.

"Tensions are high this holiday season," Lola said. She walked toward Tommy and wrapped an arm around his lower back, huddling against him. Her eyes peered around Everett and found Charlotte's in the back room. "You all right in there, Miss Wedding Planner?"

"She's in the middle of planning its demise," Everett said as he tore through another bit of croissant. "I've never seen someone want to fail so badly. She thinks it'll get more press that way."

"Don't jinx me," Charlotte said, giggling as she shot up from the bed to join the others. As she walked past her phone, several more messages from Ursula rang in. For the moment, she would ignore them. Ursula would have her full attention later.

Chapter Eleven

Everett had been in the game long enough to know that it wasn't always so easy to meet someone new.

No, that wasn't exactly it.

In actuality, it was easy to meet someone new. There were hundreds of thousands of people new all around you at any given point. These people always had backstories, jobs, families, cats, dogs, favorite songs, favorite books, and favorite foods they hated most of all. Everett ran into someone-news all the time, at bookstores, at concerts, and at events he was hired to photograph.

The rare thing about it all was meeting a new person who made you feel like the self you always wanted to feel.

To put this more plainly: Everett never felt like himself. He always felt a little like an outsider, even in his own body. No matter how many people liked him or wanted to befriend him, no matter how many jobs he got or phone numbers he was given, he never felt completely whole.

But the moment he peered into Charlotte's eyes, something

had clicked into place. The light in that empty space had turned on.

He had known exactly what jokes to make.

He had known exactly what to say.

He had watched her bloom before him, as though, all that time, she'd been waiting for him in that little spare bedroom.

The wedding planner.

Charlotte.

What a gorgeous name.

Unsure of what to do, Everett collected a handful of M&M's and sat again in the corner near Audrey. He hardly ate them, and the colors of them stained his fingers and palm. Charlotte snuck out of the room and whispered something in a girl's ear, one who looked to be around fourteen or fifteen years old.

"Abby? Gail?" the girl said. "Would you mind helping me set the table?"

"There they go. Our servants," Susan said, teasing them.

The girls set to work. Everett heard them muttering about which side the salad fork went on and where to put the napkins. There were so many of them there for dinner that the larger guy, Tommy, came over to place another leaf in the table. This led to even more conversations about where to put the extra chairs and plates. By the time the table was set, Everett's stomach had set up a little performance of backflips. He was hungry.

Lucky for him, Everett found a way through the bubbling family and sat beside Charlotte at the dinner table. Charlotte adjusted in her chair and clutched her hands together anxiously. Everett wondered if he was the one who made her nervous. He didn't want that. Or did he? It was certainly interesting, this tension brewing between them.

"Shall we pray?" Trevor, Charlotte's father, asked from the head of the table, which he shared with Wes.

Everyone bowed their heads. It had been a long time since Everett had heard a prayer. His mother wasn't the most religious, and she had slowly faded prayer out of their dinners after his father's death.

"Everlasting Father," Trevor began, "We come to you today more thankful than yesterday. You've gifted us with countless blessings over the previous year. You've watched over Susan throughout her diagnosis and treatment. You've brought all three of the Sheridan sisters back to the island after twenty-some years away. You've given my daughter, Charlotte, prosperity in the wake of disaster. You've honored Steven's son, Jonathon, with a beautiful new marriage. You've given Audrey the gift of life."

At this, Everett was pretty sure he heard Audrey snort. It wasn't like a college-aged student to give thanks for an accidental pregnancy, he supposed.

"And you've blessed Christine with the ability to be a mother through helping Audrey," Trevor continued. "Beyond that, you've brought Stan Ellis and his stepson, Tommy, into our lives. They're some of the kindest people we've ever met. They complete our lives much more than we could have fathomed. We ask you, Lord, to continue to bless my brother-in-law, Wes, as he continues on with his treatment and refines his mind each and every day. Thank you, dear Lord, for the mother of my beautiful children, my darling Kerry—and give our best to Anna up there in heaven. Tell her we miss her, we love her, and we're doing everything we can to keep this world spinning down here. Amen."

Woah. When Everett opened his eyes, he witnessed nearly every member of the extended family on the verge of tears. Trevor's wife, Kerry, placed a hand on her husband's shoulder and whispered, "That was beautiful, Trevor. Thank you."

Everyone else murmured their agreement.

After a strange pause, Trevor extended his arm toward

Everett and said, "Goodness! I forgot to add. Thank you, oh Lord, for bringing a stranger into our midst. For it's only with a stranger by your side that you realize there are no strangers in this life at all. Only people you haven't met yet."

"Thank you," Everett said sheepishly. "That means a lot."

Dinner was served. Zach looked on proudly as everyone dug into the turkey, which was seasoned perfectly and not even too dry, the stuffing, the cranberry sauce, the dinner rolls, the sweet potatoes, and the kale salad. Admittedly, most everyone avoided the kale salad altogether. Everett placed a bit of it on his plate, paying homage to his California existence. *I'll get back to you later, kale.*

Conversation bubbled on freely, as did the wine-pouring. Throughout it all, Everett thought back to Trevor's prayer. What exactly had he meant about Charlotte's disaster? It stood to reason, he supposed, that something had happened to her husband? Something like that? Although, when she threw her head back in beautiful laughter, she looked light and free, nothing like the kind of woman who'd lost her husband.

Of course, grief came in a number of different packages.

Susan made a loud "mmm" sound as she tore through her stuffing with a fork. "I am so glad my appetite came back after all that stupid chemo. This is some of the best Thanksgiving food I've ever had."

"True," her daughter, Amanda, chimed in. "We always did okay back in Newark, but this really takes the cake."

"You were living in Newark before this?" Everett asked.

Susan nodded. Her eyes shone with happiness. "I lived in Newark from age eighteen, up until June of this year."

"That's a long time," Everett said.

"My babies still live there, although I would love to get them back here," Susan said. "Speaking of babies, where are the twins?" She turned toward Kristen, her daughter-in-law.

"They finally passed out upstairs," Kristen said.

"This is the first meal I've eaten in a long time where I haven't been covered in toddler food," Susan's son, Jake, said.

"I remember those days," Lola said with a funny laugh.

"Me too," Charlotte said. She reached across the table and squeezed her daughter's wrist. "Rachel was never so messy, though. She was always ladylike."

"Ha." Rachel's cheeks burned with embarrassment.

"What about you, Everett? Any kids of your own?" Trevor asked.

Everett shook his head. "Never got around to it, I'm afraid."

"You must have quite a career," Trevor said.

"Something like that."

"He's traveled all over the world taking photographs," Christine said, lifting her glass of wine. "I Googled you. That photo you had featured in *National Geographic*..."

"Wow. Even I know that magazine," Trevor said.

"That was a long time ago," Everett said. He palmed his neck, suddenly sheepish. "I traveled to Peru for a story with a journalist I was friends with at the time. We got some great shots that day. It was only the first of two times I was featured in *National Geographic*. I mostly make money photographing events, weddings, and parties that really rich people throw."

"Like this one?" Trevor said, stretching his arms out toward the holiday before them.

Everyone laughed. But suddenly, Everett stood, walked toward his camera bag, and positioned his camera up toward his chest. Everyone looked at him like deer in headlights.

"Do you mind? You all look fantastic. And the photo will turn out better if there's still some food on your plates," Everett said.

"He knows us too well already," Claire affirmed.

"Very well. Take it," Trevor said.

Everyone became very quiet and smiled. This was the problem with photographing people: they never knew how to act naturally unless you made sure you took the photo when they weren't watching. Still, the photo turned out very nice: a portrait of many, many people who mostly all looked vaguely alike, beautiful in their own right, all simmering with love and compassion for one another.

After dinner, Christine asked if anyone was ready for pie. The collective groan was louder than a plane engine.

"Let's take a walk first," Lola suggested.

"It's not that we don't want to eat your pie, Christine," Susan said delicately. "It's just that we don't want to explode while doing it."

"Okayyyy," Christine said.

"Maybe we could head into the woods for a walk? I've been meaning to check out the birds today," Wes said. He rubbed his palms together with anticipation, his eyes sparkling.

Everyone agreed it sounded like a good idea. Everett watched as Charlotte glanced back toward the bedroom. As everyone hustled up to grab their coats and shoved their feet into snow boots, Everett nudged Charlotte and said, "I hope you're not thinking about heading back in there to do some work."

Charlotte blushed. "I just need to call her back."

"Is there any reason to call her besides easing her crazy mind?"

"No. I guess not. I have everything arranged. And if everything goes as planned, there won't be anything to worry about," Charlotte said. "She's just panicked and taking it all out on me."

"That's what I thought," he said. "And it's not fair."

Charlotte pressed her hands over her cheeks and blinked down at her half-eaten plate. Obviously, she had been too nervous to finish her food as the rest of them had.

"Just a short walk," he said. "Through the woods. It sounds so beautiful. And I don't think I could do it without you."

Charlotte arched her brow playfully. "And why not?"

Everett shrugged. "Because I'm afraid of nature. I'm a city boy. Isn't that obvious?"

Charlotte gave him a begrudging, "Fine," then stood to grab her coat with the others. As she pulled her red gloves over her hands, she blinked at him and said, "You don't have anything warm to wear, do you?"

Everett admitted he didn't. Everyone made a big fuss about this, which was exactly what Everett hadn't wanted. Susan ruffled through the back closet until she dragged out one of Wes's old hunting coats, which looked ridiculous on Everett.

"You'll look the part of Martha's Vineyard in no time," Charlotte said teasingly.

"It is warm. I'll give it that," Everett said.

"I haven't worn that coat since the winter of 1977," Wes announced.

"I swear. Your memory works in mysterious ways, Dad," Susan said as she wrapped her arm around him and nestled her head against his upper arm.

She and Wes walked up ahead of Everett and Charlotte, which allowed Charlotte to say, "You can probably guess that it's been a traumatic year in our family."

"I guess so."

"Susan had breast cancer. She's in remission now and slowly growing that gorgeous head of hair back. She keeps complaining about the streaks of silver in it, but I think she looks beautiful," Charlotte said.

"Agreed," Everett said. "She looks proud. Confident."

"Like a woman who's been through hell and came out the other side," Charlotte agreed.

Everett glanced her way again, wondering about the disaster that had befallen her life.

Of course, Charlotte chose instead to linger on everyone else's stories instead of her own. She explained about Wes's dementia, Anna's death way back in 1993, Audrey's baby and her decision to have Christine raise her until she graduated from Penn State, along with Christine's newfound love for Zach, her previous high school nemesis.

"It's so much drama," Everett finally said with a laugh as they neared the edge of the woods. Their feet crunched at the top of the snow, then slid through to the soft white snow below.

"It's been a lot to keep up with," Charlotte agreed.

"I guess it makes for a lot of things to be thankful for," he said.

She glanced at him and held his gaze for a long moment. Just then, Wes whispered harshly, "Everyone! Look! There's that cardinal up in the tree yonder. Do you see him? He sees us. He doesn't know what to make of us. But isn't he the most beautiful thing you've ever seen?"

Chapter Twelve

Hours later, Charlotte still managed to resist the allure of her phone, just beyond the spare bedroom door. Sometimes, when she caught a glimpse of it, the little light told her, *Come find me! Fix this! Put out this fire!* But each time, she turned her head back and fell again into reckless banter with Everett Rainey.

"That's way too much!" she cried now, watching as Everett smeared a full slice of apple and a full slice of pumpkin pie onto her plate.

"You can't get through Thanksgiving Day without having two slices of pie, Charlotte. Come on," he told her.

"The man has a point," Claire said from the couch, where she feasted on two slices, as well.

"You're crazy. All of you," Charlotte said. "Hey!" she exclaimed as Everett filled up her glass of wine yet again. "You know I have to work tonight."

"And I'm trying my hardest to make you forget about that," Everett said, giving her another one of his crooked smiles.

"Sabotage," she said, lifting her glass and giving him a fake-dirty look.

"And yet, here you go, drinking it all over again," Everett said. "It's too easy."

Rachel slinked up and added a slice of pumpkin pie to her dessert plate. Charlotte realized that she had spent most of the past hour talking to Everett and Everett alone. She tapped a napkin across her lips and said, "Rachel! Have you met Everett yet?"

"Not really," Rachel replied. "Hey. I'm this one's daughter."

"I can see the resemblance," Everett said good-naturedly.

"What do you think of Martha's Vineyard?" Rachel asked.

Charlotte was always so proud of how thoughtful her daughter was. Most teenagers (herself included, she thought) would have shrugged and walked away rather than drumming up a conversation.

"I haven't seen much of it, to be honest," Everett said. "I just arrived last night, met your Aunt Lola and Aunt Christine at a bar, then collapsed at the Sunrise Cove Inn. I guess I have a lot of exploring to do, although I don't know how much I'll manage since the rehearsal dinner is already tomorrow."

Rachel scrunched her nose. "It's going to be such a mess. Ursula is a real... character."

"Character is one word for it," Everett said. "I photographed her once at the Oscars. She insulted almost every other photographer in line with me."

"Not you?" Charlotte asked.

"For some reason, she gave me a pass," Everett said. "I'll never know why. To be honest, I'm sure she had an insult ready to hurl at me, but then she had to move on down the red carpet."

Rachel giggled. Charlotte slipped her fork through the cinnamon-baked apples and placed a few of them across her tongue. She closed her eyes at the perfect cinnamon-y sweetness.

"Christine. You've outdone yourself," she said. "If that cake is anything like this..."

Christine scoffed. "Yeah, right. I took ages on that cake. If that cake isn't one thousand times better than this apple pie, then I'll eat my hand."

"Baby, I love your hand. Don't eat it," Zach said playfully.

Just after eight-thirty, Charlotte admitted that she had to return home to continue work. Susan groaned and said, "You promised you wouldn't work today!"

At this, Everett said, "Admittedly, I already found her hard at work in the spare bedroom."

"Charlotte! You didn't," Susan said, feigning anger.

"I can't believe you tattled on me," Charlotte said. Fluidly, she wrapped a scarf round and round her neck, capturing her long tresses beneath. Her heart bulged in her chest, proof that she *felt something*. Then again, maybe it was just the wine.

Everett lifted his hands and said, "I would never tell a lie. Not on Thanksgiving."

"What about Valentine's Day?" Audrey said from the living area, where she was hard at work on what seemed to be her third piece of pie.

"Never," Everett said. At this, his cheeks brightened to a funny shade of pink.

A silence widened between them. They studied one another for a long moment. Charlotte couldn't believe it: she had just spent the previous hours joking and laughing with this really handsome, really successful man like it was any other day.

And she hadn't really thought of Jason once.

What did that mean?

Did she regret that?

"I think I'll walk back to the Sunrise Cove Inn," Everett said suddenly.

In the corner, Audrey whistled.

That girl really had zero self-control.

"Oh?" Charlotte said.

"I guess that means you three will walk to town together," Susan said. "It's the same route."

"Great," Everett said.

"And Everett, I insist that you use Dad's old coat," Susan said. "Like he said, he hasn't worn the thing since the seventies. It'll get much more wear out there than it will in here." She then leaned forward to whisper, "Plus, he can't stop buying new winter clothes from catalogs. I didn't even know people ordered from catalogs anymore. Frankly, he's just as bad as a woman when it comes to shopping."

Both Everett and Charlotte laughed, both grateful to have something to think about that wasn't whatever this physical attraction was between them.

Or whatever it was.

Maybe it wasn't physical.

It had been a long time since Charlotte had made a new friend.

Maybe this was what it felt like?

Charlotte watched as both Rachel and Everett shrugged into their winter coats. Christine rushed forward to shove a plate of pie into Everett's hands.

"You probably don't have much to snack on back at the Inn. The bistro will be open tomorrow, but there won't be much going on. Zach hired a substitute to work over the wedding weekend to serve the few guests. I don't want you to go hungry." She pondered this for a moment and then added, "If you want more food, we usually keep that door wide open. We always come in and out and take from the fridge as we like. I hope you know you can do the same."

Everett looked overwhelmed. Charlotte wanted to protest, like, *Sorry, my family is so overbearing.*

But in reality, it was kind of nice, wasn't it? That her family had spread their arms so wide for this stranger?

She didn't want to belong to any other kind of family.

Outside, winter magic spread like a shimmering blanket across Martha's Vineyard. Charlotte lifted her gaze toward the moon, which was dropped low in the night sky and cast everything in bluish light.

"They really don't make nights like these out west," Everett said.

"I've never been," Charlotte said. "Maybe I don't want to."

Everett laughed. He stepped forward first, crunching through the first layer of snow. "I relish that sound," he said. "It's delicious. Like cracking the top of a crème brûlée."

"Ha. I've never thought of it like that," Charlotte admitted.

Rachel scampered up ahead, crafting her own deep footsteps in the snow. Charlotte and Everett walked behind, both wordless. Charlotte could feel it: he wanted to know why her father had mentioned that "disaster" in his prayer. He had given her away.

But she was a widow. That was her reality.

It wasn't like she wanted to hide it.

Still, it wasn't the most fun topic of conversation.

When they reached town, Everett suddenly stepped to the side, grabbed a big bunch of snow, formed a super-compact snowball, and whacked it against Charlotte's stomach.

It all happened so quickly that Charlotte only had time to scream.

Rachel whipped around at the sound and looked at them, bug-eyed. After a long, frozen moment, both Charlotte and Everett burst into laughter.

Suddenly, the war began.

It was every man for him or herself.

Charlotte rushed toward the post office, where she drew together the first of many snowballs, spun around, and smashed a ball directly into Rachel's back. Rachel hollered and turned to splash her mother with her own snowball. By the time it registered, Charlotte already had another ball prepared. She ran headlong toward Everett, making wild sounds, and then nabbed him on the upper bicep.

"Hey! I think that had ice in it!" Everett cried.

"Wait, really?" Charlotte's pulse quickened.

"No." At that, Everett shot a perfect snowball toward her; it smashed against her leg and disintegrated.

"You tricked me!" Charlotte said.

"Ha! Sucker!" Everett said.

The snowball fight went on another ten minutes or so until the three of them stood, gasping for air with their hands on their knees.

"I forgot how tough it is to run through the snow," Everett admitted.

"Yeah. I'm exhausted," Charlotte said.

"Too exhausted to work, maybe?" Everett said sneakily.

"Naw." Charlotte laughed. "But good try."

"Ha. Well." Everett glanced back toward the Sunrise Cove Inn. "I guess I'd better head back."

"Sure. Everything okay there? You're the only guest?"

"For the time being, yeah," he said. "And it's fun. A big, creaky inn, all to myself. Now that would be one hell of a Stephen King book."

"Don't let the ghosts bite," Charlotte said.

Everett held her gaze for a moment. "Thanks for a beautiful Thanksgiving. I guess I'll see you tomorrow before the rehearsal dinner."

"Indeed," Charlotte said. "Let the games begin."

"You're going to kill it," he told her. "I've never seen anyone more capable."

Rachel and Charlotte turned to walk the rest of the way to their house. Charlotte buzzed with anticipation. They had walked for a full two minutes in silence before Rachel said, *"I've never seen anyone more capable,"* in a voice that clearly resembled Everett's darker one.

"What? He's kind," Charlotte said with a shrug.

"He likes you. I've never seen anyone crush so hard since Abby with this kid in art class," Rachel teased.

"Don't be silly. We're working together. We're basically in the same business. It's good to meet new friends," Charlotte insisted.

"I would tell you you're being delusional, but I think you already know that," Rachel retorted.

"Where do you come up with this stuff?"

Back inside, Charlotte brewed them some cups of hot cocoa while Rachel snapped on a chick flick and burrowed herself in blankets on the couch. Charlotte checked her various messages, mostly from Ursula, Tobias, and Ursula's mother.

> URSULA: I just got word from the quintet. Apparently, they're going to make it after all. Can you plz confirm?

> URSULA: Charlotte? I need your go-ahead before I press play on these shoes. I wanted to wear these other ones, but what do you think of these?

> URSULA: I went ahead and bought both pairs. You can help me decide when I arrive tomorrow.

> URSULA: Finally, back in New York. Guess we're on track. We are going to take all these supplements to beat the jet lag!

> URSULA: Omg, Orion is being so difficult about his tux. I swear, men are such idiots, right?

> URSULA: Are you getting these, Charlotte?

> URSULA: CHARLOTTE?

> URSULA: Okay. Call me when you get this.

Charlotte called Ursula at that moment, but the call went straight to voicemail. Nothing Ursula, Tobias, or the mother of the bride had sent seemed pressing. They had just seemed like overly-anxious messages, the kinds people sent a couple days before a huge, multi-million-dollar wedding.

Everything was in place.

Everything would be fine.

She had to believe it.

In a very strange way, having Everett tell her that had made her believe it even more.

She settled in beside Rachel with her hot cocoa. Rachel gave her an incredulous look.

"You're already done?"

Charlotte shrugged. "I think it can wait till morning. All parties are headed our way. Tomorrow, Martha's Vineyard will explode."

"Ha. And you think you'll be able to sleep tonight?" Rachel asked.

"Of course not," Charlotte said with an ironic laugh. "But I'll close my eyes and pray to God above that everything will go smoothly."

"What do you think of Everett?" Rachel asked then.

"Not this again."

"I'm just curious," she said. "I don't know." She swallowed another gulp of hot cocoa, then added, "He makes snowballs almost as good as Dad."

Charlotte's heart sank. "Yes. He does."

"But Dad's hurt more," Rachel said. "Or maybe I was just younger, so I thought they hurt more."

It was their second winter without him. Both of them stewed in this fact for a moment, staring blankly at the rom-com as it whipped from one dramatic plot to another. Charlotte's throat constricted.

"You know what your dad thought of rom coms?" she asked.

Rachel shook her head. A tear trickled down her cheek, but she didn't make any motion to brush it off.

"He said that they were silly. And you know what? Every single time I convinced him to watch one, he complained about it for the first fifteen minutes, and then, by the end of it, he was mopping up his tears," Charlotte said, smiling to herself.

"That's ridiculous," Rachel replied.

"I know. And he always made me promise never to tell anyone. Can you imagine what would have happened if one of his fishermen buddies had heard?"

"They would have never let him hear the end of it," Rachel affirmed with a laugh. She squeezed her eyes shut again, then forced them open again. Tears lined her cheeks. "Thank you for telling me that. It changes him a little bit, but in a good way."

"I'll give you as many memories as I can of him, for as long as I can," Charlotte said. "It's all we can do to keep him with us."

Before she turned out the light for the night, Charlotte blinked again at the old closet, still stocked full of Jason's old coats and shirts. She ran her fingers over the old flannel, inhaling the last lingering scent of that horrible fish.

"I still love you, you know," she told the shirts, as though Jason himself could hear her.

Chapter Thirteen

*I*t was Friday: the day of reckoning.

This was what Everett wanted to text to Charlotte as a joke, if only he had taken her number. As it stood, he was all alone, a cup of coffee in hand and a piece of leftover pie on a plate there in the Sunrise Cove Inn. He watched the Sound as it shifted beneath the suddenly vibrant, winter blue sky, the kind that made it almost painful to look down at the snow. It was the sort of weather that would have allowed any plane in the world to land peacefully on that airstrip toward the southeastern part of the island.

This meant that everyone from the string quintet to Ursula Pennington herself would arrive without a problem.

Everett lined up his various lenses for the day, making little notes to himself about the celebrities he needed to include in photographs, as promised to his editor at *Wedding Today*. Before he knew it, he had constructed a whole page full of notes and also eaten one and a half slices of apple pie. Again, he glanced at his phone with the thought that he should call his mother.

Again, he retreated from this idea.

He didn't want to ruin his good mood.

The rehearsal dinner was set for eight in the evening. According to Charlotte, the day before, Ursula had insisted that she didn't want to actually "rehearse" the wedding itself. "She made something up about it being bad luck," Charlotte had said, scrunching that cute nose of hers. "Like, I just know something is going to go wrong on the day of because she basically insists on this."

"What's the point of a rehearsal dinner without the rehearsal itself?" Everett had asked.

"Good question. I guess, in her mind, it's just more time to hobnob with all these celebrities coming to the island. It's just another reason to drink champagne at a thousand dollars a pop." She had zipped her lips and resigned to Ursula's ways. "I just want to make it out of the weekend alive and in one piece."

"Alive? Maybe. Missing an arm? Also a maybe," Everett had teased her.

Everett decided to go for a walk through the snow that afternoon as a means to get his head screwed on correctly before the event that night. He was surprised to find the town bustling, as it had been more-or-less quiet the day before. He grabbed a cup of coffee at a little coffeehouse and watched as a young mother led her two toddlers across the little square, headed toward the antique carousel.

Everett hired a taxi to take him to the mansion near Edgartown, which Charlotte had booked for both the rehearsal dinner and the wedding and reception the following day. The taxi driver filled him in on several facts about the old mansion, like how only ten or so celebrities had ever been married there, as it was difficult to reserve it. "The owners are pretty specific about who they allow getting married there. My hunch is that it's because Charlotte Hamner is the wedding planner. They love the Montgomery and Sheridan girls over there. The whole island does."

"I think I might have met them," Everett said with a smile.

"Oh? That's great. Treasure that. They don't make a lot of 'em like that anymore," the driver said.

At the mansion, Everett stood in the snow, wearing that ridiculous hunting coat from the seventies, and took several photos of the exterior. The place echoed "winter wonderland" in almost every single way. It looked as though it had been taken from the top of the French Alps and dropped right there, at the edge of the Sound.

Suddenly, another taxi yanked up behind him.

"Hey, stranger."

He turned to find Audrey, the pregnant daughter of Lola, drawing herself out slowly from the back of the taxi. The taxi driver hustled around and blared, "Audrey! I told you that I would help you out. For goodness sake, why don't you ever listen?"

Audrey rolled her eyes. "I'm getting abuse from all sides." She then removed several bills from her pocket and placed them in the driver's hand. "Thank you for the ride and for changing the radio station. You know how I feel about disco." She scrunched up her nose.

Everett had to laugh. The taxi driver shook his head violently and muttered something about, "Women in your condition," before sitting back in the driver's seat and rolling through the snow.

"Sorry about that," Audrey said and shrugged her shoulders.

"No worries. Always a pleasure to watch you make someone else uncomfortable."

"What can I say? It's something of a specialty."

"Are you helping with the decorations?" Everett asked.

"To be honest with you, I think I might have missed most of

it," Audrey said. "My mother will be mad about it, but she'll only give me five minutes' worth of a hard time before she completely forgets."

Everett laughed good-naturedly. He adjusted his camera strap around his neck. "Shall we?"

"I guess it's time to join the chaos," she agreed.

Together, they walked up the stone path toward the entrance of the mansion. When they reached the door, they heard Zach in the midst of what sounded to be a raucous fight with one of his staff members.

"I don't know why you would ever, ever stir up a sauce like that, Marty! I mean, didn't I train you well enough? Look at it. It's already curdled on top. You have to start over..."

Audrey and Everett exchanged panicked glances.

This particular door spit them into a corridor near the kitchen. When they entered, Christine popped out of the kitchen door and gave them a bug-eyed look.

"There you are," she said.

"Sorry I'm late," Audrey said.

"No worries. We've had plenty of help. Come on! It looks fantastic so far," Christine said.

They followed Christine down the corridor, left, then right, until they fell into a glorious old-world ballroom, one with enormous ceilings that featured an elaborate mural. In awe, Everett lifted his camera and took several photos, hardly remembering to line them up. He hadn't seen anything so beautiful since his last stint in Europe, more than five years before.

The ballroom itself was decorated elaborately, yet tastefully: exactly the way *Wedding Today* liked. White tablecloths were hung across long tables; chandeliers hung over them, glittering with soft light; and a Christmas tree was dressed to the nines in the center of the room, detailed with what looked like diamond "ice." Given the expense of the wedding, Everett would have bet his bottom dollar the ice was made of actual diamonds.

Audrey reappeared without her coat. She wore a black dress, which bulged out beautifully over her pregnant belly. She walked toward the Christmas tree and blinked up toward the angel on top. The view was gorgeous: a new mother on the verge of something else. Everett took a quick photo of her, hoping to give it to her later.

But Audrey, being Audrey, caught him in the act.

"What did you just do?" she demanded, stomping toward him.

Everett was at a loss for what to say. "I um..."

"Let me see it," Audrey said. "I can decide whether or not you should delete it. I'm pretty self-conscious about the old belly, you know. I don't know if I want to remember my fat years."

"Ha. Okay. It's a deal," he said.

He passed his camera to her so she could flick through the last several, all of which featured her. Immediately, her face changed. Her eyebrows lowered.

For a long moment, Everett thought she might throw the camera on the ground with anger.

But when she lifted her face again, her eyes glittered with tears.

"I've never seen myself like that before," she said.

Everett was at a loss for words.

"I look just like my mother when she was pregnant with me," Audrey said. "I've heard people say it, of course—but I've never seen it so clearly. I..." She bit hard on her lower lip as she passed the camera back to Everett. "I can see why you're as sought-after as you are. You're clearly fantastic. Thank you."

Before Everett could find an answer, Charlotte burst into the ballroom. She wore a glorious burgundy gown, cut low over her breasts and billowing out behind her thin waist and killer legs. Her brunette loose curls wafted behind her shoulders, pinned up halfway. Everett's heart tap-danced across his chest. He lifted his camera again and snapped a photo. When he glanced at it in the reel, however, he realized it would be difficult to fully capture the light behind Charlotte's eyes.

"Thank you for your hard work today, everyone," she announced to the decorators, her family, and her friends. "It means the world to me, especially given the last-minute nature of this whole affair. But our first guests have already begun to arrive, which means I need you to take all your coats to the coatroom; I need Audrey and Amanda in the coatroom itself to take guests' things; I need all busboys and servers to report to Zach, and I need—you—" She pointed toward Everett and beckoned. "To come with me."

Everett could have pinched himself.

He stepped toward Charlotte and fell into stride with her as they marched back toward the proper entrance, where limousines hummed, filled with celebrities and rich folk, all in designer dresses and snapping selfies. The only thing celebrities liked more than professional photos taken of them was photos they took of themselves.

At least, this was what Everett had noticed over the years.

"You okay?" he asked Charlotte as she sauntered through the door to greet the first approaching guests.

"Better than ever," Charlotte said brightly.

"Really?" Everett asked as he lifted the camera.

Charlotte's eyes glittered. "No, you idiot. I'm barely treading water."

With that, she winked at him, then shot out the door with her arms outstretched. "Ursula! Welcome to Martha's Vineyard. You look more beautiful than ever."

She did. Everett stepped out into the chilly air and lifted his camera to capture the first snaps of this blond, leggy bombshell on the eve of her wedding to one of the most famous basketball stars in the world. Ursula bent down and kissed Charlotte's cheeks—something she had probably picked up during her stint in Sicily.

Following her was a wide variety of her entourage: women Everett recognized from both high-caliber and low-caliber TV shows, musicians who had some acclaim in the pop and R&B world, men who made indie films, that sort of thing. Everyone was dressed immaculately and commenting on the snow, as though it was just a prop.

"It's gorgeous. Have you ever seen it so thick before?" one girl asked, her voice bright as she snapped several photos of herself with the snowy backdrop.

"And this mansion! I mean, so chic, right?" another guy said.

Everett caught Charlotte's eye as she led Ursula into the mansion. Just before she disappeared, he mouthed, "Good luck."

She was going to need it.

Chapter Fourteen

Charlotte hadn't slept a wink.

She now found herself running on coffee and Diet Coke fumes, buzzing alongside the world-famous Ursula Pennington as they walked toward the ballroom. Ursula's topics of conversation ranged from, "I really had a lot of ideas for the wedding while in Sicily. It's too bad we have so much of it nailed down already," to, "I really wish you would have told me this mansion was so small. It really puts a wrench in our plans," to, "Do you think the snow is too much? Some people say it's too elaborate," to, "I didn't realize you were so pretty, Charlotte. I mean, for how old you are."

Charlotte already wanted to pull every single hair out of her head.

When they appeared in the ballroom, Charlotte was grateful that everyone had gone to their designated positions for the evening. Even the string quintet had set up near the Christmas tree and begun to play. They were certainly just as good as they'd advertised themselves to be. As Harvard grads, they better be.

Ursula walked slowly through the tables, analyzing the expensive china, the flowers, the Christmas tree itself, the fountain, and the sculpture toward the far end of the ballroom. She smirked, but her smile didn't extend past her face. Slowly, her friends and entourage began to stream into the ballroom after her. Servers walked out from the side doors, armed with trays filled with drinks—a fancy cocktail that Charlotte had invented for Ursula and Orion's rehearsal dinner.

"Charlotte. May I speak with you for a moment? In private," Ursula said, loud enough for several of her friends to hear.

Here we go.

"Right this way," Charlotte said brightly. She led Ursula through a double-wide set of doors toward the east, which led into a little arena she'd set aside for women with wardrobe malfunctions and sore feet. The place was parlor-like, with antique furniture, old-world paintings, and a gorgeous golden statue of a peacock.

Ursula collapsed in a heap on an antique fainting couch, which seemed fitting.

Charlotte remained standing.

"Charlotte, Charlotte, darling," Ursula said. She puckered her overly bright red lips together and made a little, horrible noise. "I don't know what I was thinking, assuming you could put together exactly what I wanted in only a few weeks."

Neither do I.

"In any case, I mean, it's absolutely fine," Ursula said, furrowing her brow. "Only that, I noticed you didn't take my flower specifications to heart? What do you mean by this?"

Charlotte remembered a number of "recommendations" from Ursula regarding flowers. The girl had changed her mind so many times that Charlotte had grown dizzy.

"My sister is the florist involved in the wedding," Charlotte said. She kept her voice up, chipper. "Would you like me to get her so that we can discuss this in better detail?"

"I don't see that that's necessary. In my mind, you're the wedding planner. Everything should have gone through you first," Ursula said. She lifted her perfectly manicured nails and tapped them against her thumb. "I suppose when my friends ask me why everything isn't absolutely stellar, I'll have to report this to them."

You mean when they finish taking selfies of themselves and gossiping? When they notice that everything isn't precisely to your liking? When will that happen? When could they ever look outside themselves?

"Perhaps I can fix this before the reception tomorrow," Charlotte said instead. She had to. This was the client, for goodness sake. "It's going to be held in the other ballroom, on the opposite side of the mansion. It's the fancier of the two, the one the original owners had built for their wedding back in the 1800s."

"How quaint," Ursula said.

If you don't like history, why did you choose to have your wedding on Martha's Vineyard?

"As long as you understand what I feel, I suppose we must move forward," Ursula said, again heaving a sigh. She glanced down at her feet in those impossibly-high six-inch heels.

You just wanted to yell at someone while you rested your feet.

"I guess I should go greet my guests. I do hope Orion gets here soon. It will be difficult to marry him if he never arrives," Ursula said with an ironic laugh.

"Did you not travel together?"

"No. I was in Sicily, as you know, and he was in LA with his teammates celebrating the last of his bachelor days."

"Right."

"Do you think he did anything really bad? Something I

wouldn't approve of?" Ursula asked suddenly. Her face clenched up. "I mean, did you read anything in the tabloids or..."

Charlotte furrowed her brow. She certainly hadn't expected this—Ursula showing just how low her self-esteem could go.

"No. Nothing like that has been reported. Just that he had a good time out west," she said.

Like I've had time to read a tabloid magazine while putting together this wedding.

"Oh, good. That's fantastic news. I wouldn't want that kind of gossip to follow me around at the rehearsal dinner," Ursula said. She then prepared a vibrant smile and popped up from the fainting couch. When she reached the doorway, she said, "I suppose the ballroom looks fine. A bit lackluster, but nothing outrageously out of line."

Charlotte lifted her hand, preparing to demand Ursula stay. She had to go through a number of things for the next hours, including the schedule of events, just to make sure Ursula knew when to head where and what happened next. As a wedding planner, she had outlined when toasts were meant to happen, when the dancing would begin, and when they had to clear the ballroom for the night.

Clearly, Ursula didn't care about that sort of thing. She bolted through the door and left Charlotte swimming in doubt and annoyance.

Rachel appeared in the crack of the doorway only a second later.

"Mom!" she called.

"Oh, God. What happened now?" Charlotte asked.

But Rachel came forward and wrapped her arms around her in answer. Charlotte placed her chin on her daughter's shoulder, suddenly overwhelmed. She could have lived in that hug forever.

"What's up?" Charlotte finally asked, unable to recognize her own voice.

Rachel drew back. She gripped her mother with hard fingers. "I heard what she said to you. I'm so mad for you. You worked so hard on this."

Charlotte closed her eyes. "I figured something like this would happen, Pumpkin. Don't worry about it, though. It's not my first rodeo."

"But she's evil. Why couldn't she just say thank you? I mean, you pulled off this incredible night. All the celebrities out there are in awe of the entire setting. I've already seen the event featured on Instagram Live like twelve times," Rachel said.

Charlotte sniffed just once, the only proof she was willing to give her daughter that she felt down in the dumps. "Then, we've done exactly what we set out to do. Ursula won't remember belittling me tonight. She'll only remember the photos that are taken, what's written about the event, that sort of thing. So it's up to us to keep going. Keep fighting—no matter what happens next."

At that moment, the speaker system was turned on. Ursula's voice barreled out of every speaker in the ballroom.

"No!" Charlotte cried. "It's too soon. The quintet is supposed to play for another hour during cocktails."

She hustled back toward the ballroom, very nearly tripping on her dress. When she reached it, she found almost every table already filled. Every shade of pink, purple, dark green, dark yellow, and burgundy blared back at her; diamond earrings glittered from nearly every ear. The perfume seemed like a kind of cloud over everything, mixing and shoving itself through Charlotte's nostrils.

Ursula stood near the Christmas tree with her beloved groom, Orion. Just as in the photographs, Orion towered over Ursula, standing with his hands behind his back and his chest puffed out. His face was either stoic or bored-looking, depending on what you thought of him.

That man does not look like he wants to get married tomorrow.

"Good evening, everyone," Ursula said brightly.

And the toasts weren't meant to begin for another hour or more.

Why the heck did I put together such an elaborate schedule if Ursula planned to come in and stomp all over it?

"Thank you for traveling all the way here to beautiful Martha's Vineyard," Ursula continued.

Okay. She hasn't said anything off the wall so far. Maybe it's okay?

"All my life, I've wanted to get married here," Ursula continued. "My mother herself got married here when she was just a little nobody. Age twenty. Didn't you, Mom?"

Ursula's mother stood and waved her hand, which glittered with four jeweled rings.

Ursula then turned her eyes toward Orion. They, too, glittered, like the rings and the earrings and the delicate detail on the Christmas tree.

"Orion, my love," she said. "I want to tell you that I love you with my whole heart. No matter what's happened in our pasts, I know that we'll be together forever. Thank you for your love and your companionship. And thank you for standing here before me today and tomorrow, in front of—four hundred of our nearest and dearest friends and family—and pledging your honor to me."

It was all a little overly dramatic. After a long pause, a few of Ursula's girlfriends smacked their hands together. Someone else wolf-whistled. Charlotte made the mistake of catching Everett's eye across the ballroom. He had been busy taking endless photographs of the celebrities, of Ursula, and of Orion.

He made a face, like, *Boy, that was awkward,* which nearly made Charlotte double-over with laughter.

Be chill. You have a job to do. No laughing until long after Ursula and Orion fly away in their private jet on their way to their honeymoon.

Charlotte grimaced toward Everett, which seemed to translate everything he wanted to know. He laughed privately for her, then straightened his face and took more photos.

It was going to be a long night. Charlotte could feel it in her bones.

The bride was unruly. The groom looked like he wanted to get the hell out of dodge. And Charlotte, herself, was on the verge of either a nervous breakdown—or falling for someone new?

No. That wasn't right.

That wasn't anything she could trust.

Chapter Fifteen

When asked about it later, Everett wasn't able to recall exactly when the rehearsal dinner party got so wildly out of control.

Dinner, for one, seemed to go off almost without a hitch. He watched as these illustrious Instagram-famous ladies, actresses, and musicians ate heartily and commented on Zach's cooking in a way that made Everett almost proud. He hadn't known the guy that long, of course—only a day! —but he'd still been able to feast on his Thanksgiving dinner beforehand.

Now, some of the richest people in the world regarded it as high-end cuisine.

That was pretty cool.

The food itself was fancy and, incredibly, mostly local—with cheeses and butter taken from the local dairy farm, salmon and crab and octopus taken from the Sound itself, bread from both Christine and the local bakery, and veal and raw beef taken from a local farm. After Everett snuck around, snapping as many photos as possible, he sat with the meal for a good ten minutes. He closed his eyes as he ate as slowly as he could—focusing on every possible flavor that hit his taste buds.

"You look like you're enjoying yourself."

His eyes popped open to find Susan: her hands on her hips and her short hair styled beautifully.

"You caught me," he said. "I really love this food. Zach's a magician."

"Something like that," Susan agreed. "Have you seen Charlotte? I can't find her, and I'm worried. The last time I saw her, I thought she was going to fall on the floor. I have doubts she got any sleep last night."

"I imagine she didn't," he said.

"What are we going to do with her?" Susan asked. "We're going to have to carry her out of here due to exhaustion in like ten minutes flat."

Everett chuckled. "She's a professional. She's probably riding high on adrenaline right now. She'll crash the minute it's over late Saturday, but not a moment before."

"I can't find my other sisters, either," Susan said. "Scott and I are tired. Charlotte probably told you, but I just finished up some treatment that knocks me out early. Will you tell Charlotte that we headed out?"

"Of course." Everett waved a hand toward Scott, who waited for Susan near the exit. "You'll be around tomorrow?"

"Wouldn't miss it for the world," Susan said.

Susan's words had a way of working through Everett's brain over the next few minutes, so much so that he finished up his meal early and set out on a hunt for Charlotte. Around this time, everyone finished up their food, shoved their plates aside, and focused on the alcohol portion of the evening. Wine, cocktails, straight hard liquor—it all flowed like water itself. Everett wondered if rich people even bothered to drink water. Maybe it was beneath them?

An actress named Zelda swept toward the front of the room

and wiggled her hips, then cast her arms toward the ceiling and said, "Let's burn this thing to the ground!" At that moment, the DJ began to blare wild beats at the turntable toward the far end of the room.

Again, Everett searched for Charlotte. This was something he at least wanted to joke with her about. At worst, he wanted to find her, just in case Susan was right, and she'd collapsed somewhere due to exhaustion.

Ursula shimmied against Zelda, then turned around and hugged her friend as hard as she could. Everett wasn't one to forget his duties. He hurriedly snapped a photo of the celebrity friends, checked it, and then snapped a second for good measure. "Get as much of the chaos as you can," his editor at *Wedding Today* had said. "Just in case we can extend our 'fancy wedding spread' to the 'party' section."

Everett marched away from Ursula after that, past the groom's friends, who all surrounded him and spoke to him with downturned, stoic faces. They didn't look like the kind of guys who wanted their friend to get married. Was it because it was the end of an era? Or was there something more sinister at play?

When Everett got to the kitchen, he found himself at the mercy of another Zach fight.

Worried the words he spewed were directed toward Charlotte, he charged through the door to find Zach, Christine, Lola, and some other guy he didn't recognize, who had been hired to help serve for the night. Lola wavered on her heels, clearly drunk, while Christine kept her arm around Lola, maybe to keep them both upright.

"I don't think you can just charge in here, help me serve my top-grade dishes all night, and then tell me that I'm morally corrupt because I'm not a vegan," Zach blared.

"I've gone through all the facts with you," the man

returned. "The environmental impact. The morality. Every-thing. And you still won't see reason."

Lola turned toward Everett, grinned broadly, and then rolled her eyes.

"Dude! I don't know why you think you have an audience here. All I'm going to do is point you toward the door," Zach returned. His cheeks grew redder and redder.

"Seems like I walked into something I shouldn't have," Everett said under his breath toward Lola.

"Oh, yeah. And it's just now getting good. It all started because Zach wanted him to help him prep for tomorrow. He was like—I won't touch that! Insane," Lola said, shaking her head. "I just wish I had some popcorn for the show."

"Besides. You've stood here arguing with me for so long, you forgot your dessert duties!" Zach howled.

"I love when he's like this," Christine whispered to Everett. "He's such a sweetie to me, but I like to see his dark side every now and then."

Although Everett appreciated the show, he needed to find Charlotte. He asked them if they'd seen her at all.

"Nope," Lola said. "Maybe she ran away? I might have if I had to deal with that horrible Ursula woman. You know, Rachel told me that Ursula pinned Charlotte in that side parlor earlier and reprimanded her about the decorations?"

"What?" Everett demanded.

"Yep. I'm sure it was just to put Charlotte in her place or something. But still. The nerve of this woman! Charlotte has gone above and beyond to make this night special."

"And to think. We're only on night one of two," Christine said somberly.

Everett thanked them for their help, then shot out into the ballroom again. He nearly staggered directly into Rachel, who seemed in the middle of a hefty flirt session with someone she introduced as Orion's cousin. Like Orion, the teenager was headed toward seven feet tall.

"He doesn't play basketball, though. He's into baseball," Rachel said proudly.

"That's great. America's pastime." Everett cleared his throat. It wasn't that he didn't care; it was just that he had bigger fish to fry. As if any fish in a party like this would ever go near a fryer.

"Have you seen your mom?"

"Not lately," Rachel said absently, her eyes turned toward Orion's cousin's bored-looking hazel ones. "I'm sure she's just busy."

Everett hustled across the ballroom, nearly toppling over a congo line, which resulted in several actresses scream-crying overly dramatically. Probably, they always thought there was an agent nearby, waiting to cast them in some film.

When Everett reached the parlor where Christine and Lola had suggested Charlotte was, he stopped short.

Sure enough, he heard Ursula's voice on the other side of the thick, ornate door.

"I have never seen a party get so out-of-hand," Ursula said. Her voice broke a bit. It wavered between crying and scream-ing. "And you know, the first moment I saw you, Charlotte—I knew that you couldn't handle something like this. I knew that I had given the job to the wrong woman. I knew that you—"

Everett didn't know what came over him.

He only knew that—famous woman or not, Charlotte's client or not, the very woman who had once won two Oscars in back-to-back years, defeating the likes of Susan Sarandon and Meryl Streep—nobody would talk to Charlotte that way.

He couldn't allow it.

He burst through the door, lifted his camera, and, without thinking, snapped a photo of Ursula.

Ursula looked like she had been involved in some kind of accident.

Black ink streaked her cheeks and the area around her eyes. Her lipstick had smeared all the way down her chin and appeared on the backs of her hands. Her hair was all mussed, the curls falling over her cheeks and over her ears, and she actually shook with either rage or sadness or both.

In contrast, beside her, Charlotte stood pristine as ever. She looked like the famous one, in Everett's eyes: beautiful, regal, her shoulders back and her chin lifted to look up at the horrendous woman who yelled at her.

After Everett snapped the photo, Ursula turned horrified eyes toward him.

She looked at him like he had just shot her.

"What. Did. You. Just. Do," Ursula growled at him.

She looked a lot like one of the roles she had gotten an Oscar for, actually—the one where she had played a mother who had been on a drunken rampage, whose young children had been taken away from her. Everett had taken a date to the film during another stint in LA. Neither of them had liked the movie; neither of them had liked the other person, either.

Everett lifted the camera in the silence. Ursula looked on the verge of tearing him apart with her bare hands.

"Listen to me very carefully," Everett said. He was surprised to find that he sounded articulate and clear-headed. "If you don't stop berating your wedding planner, I will send this photo to TMZ in five seconds flat. Everyone will know what a crazy bridezilla you are."

Ursula placed her hands on her hips. Her lower lip bubbled around for a second like she was a toddler who hadn't gotten her way. Charlotte's eyes scanned him, then Ursula, then back. Ursula collapsed on the little fainting couch with her head in her hands.

"Just make me look pretty again," she howled into her palms.

Charlotte and Everett again shared a moment. Charlotte looked on the verge of either tears or endless laughter. Everett felt on the verge of wrapping her in a big hug, dotting a kiss on her forehead, and...

No. He couldn't think about that. Not now.

"Just let me put this woman back together," Charlotte said softly.

"*This woman?*" Ursula cried. "Did she really just call me that? I'm beloved—" She hiccupped, then, only adding insult to it all.

"Just do what Charlotte tells you to do, and the world won't see this photo," Everett said.

God, he had never felt so much power in all his life.

Charlotte shooed him toward the door. He shrugged and mouthed, *Let me know if you need anything else?* And she nodded and rolled her eyes.

When he returned to the hallway, he clipped the door closed and listened for a moment as Ursula howled with tears.

"I'm so sorry!" she cried.

You had to feel a bit bad for her, he guessed. All that pressure. All that fame.

Sure—the money would have been nice.

By the time he reached the ballroom again, the party had reached more dramatic heights. A musician he recognized reared a beer bottle back, then smashed it across the ground and said, "Monica! I told you to stop CALLING me that!"

Everett caught sight of Lola, Tommy, Christine, and Zach on the other side of the ballroom. Rachel appeared beside Lola, her eyes buggy. How had they lost such control? Lola beckoned for Everett to join them. He did and huddled beside them, at a complete loss of what to do.

"It's barely midnight," Lola breathed.

"Maybe Charlotte will know what to do," Everett said.

"Where is she?"

"Almost ready, I think. There was a little snag in the parlor with Ursula."

"Did she yell at her again?" Rachel demanded.

Luckily, the few security staff members they had hired for the event hustled toward the man who had thrown the beer bottle and gave him a stern talking to. Another member of staff rushed toward the glass, made a perimeter, and began to sweep it up. Still, everyone seemed oddly manic; the air shivered with tension.

At that moment, Charlotte and Ursula appeared on the other side of the ballroom. Ursula looked very nearly cleaned up but still a little ragged. Charlotte sliced a finger across her neck and shook her head.

"Nothing good happens in this crowd after midnight," Tommy affirmed. "Let's get them out of here."

Chapter Sixteen

Charlotte couldn't believe what Everett had done for her.

He had risked his own career and the wedding itself.

And miraculously, the plan had worked.

Now, Ursula stood beside her a broken woman: no longer the demanding "famous actress" she had been moments before. It had been oddly sweet when Ursula had allowed Charlotte to put together the pieces of her beautiful face: mopping up the eyeliner and drawing fresh lines, cleaning up the lipstick and adding it to her unique, large lips.

"They're fake," Ursula informed her as she hiccupped again.

"That's okay," Charlotte had said, furrowing her brow in concentration.

"I just. I never wanted my face to be made of plastic. But there's so much pressure on you in this industry," Ursula continued. Another tear streaked down through the eyeliner Charlotte had only just drawn.

Now, out in the ballroom itself, Charlotte watched as Everett walked across the ballroom, lifted the microphone that was attached to the speaker system, and announced, "Good evening, everyone. It looks to me like tonight got us off to a fabulous start for the marriage between Ursula and Orion. Congratulations!"

Some of the guests clapped and howled with laughter. Specifically, the guy who security had taken off to the side yelped with excitement, having apparently created some kind of chaos. What had he done? Charlotte had only gotten the security guards as a precaution. She hadn't actually thought they would be necessary.

"I believe many of you are staying in this very mansion tonight," Everett said. "Although I'll leave that up to you. The rest of you with hotels and BnBs booked in Edgartown and Oak Bluffs, call your limo drivers up and head out. It's a beautiful night out there—one rife for whatever madness you want to get into in the comfort of your own hotel rooms. Good night, every-one. And we'll see you in the other ballroom tomorrow!"

Everett's eyes connected with Charlotte's over the sea of grumbling partygoers. He gave a light shrug as she mouthed, *Thank you. Again.* Already, it felt like they could communicate without words, even across hundreds of people.

Orion himself appeared beside Charlotte, wrapped his arm around Ursula, and said, "Let's get you to bed."

This was the first act of any sort of love Charlotte had seen out of the weekend's groom, which warmed her heart. She watched for a moment as Orion and Ursula kind of limped toward the corridor, which led toward the staircase that wrapped up and up, grandly, in a circle, toward the separate suites Charlotte had booked for them. She hadn't had time to show Ursula where they were, but she had instructed Rachel to show them to Orion. She was grateful to see that had actually happened.

As a wedding planner, it was essential that all the pieces of the puzzle fell into place at the right time.

Right now, however, she felt as though most of the pieces of the puzzle remained on the floor, covered in mud.

It wasn't going to be easy to get all these intoxicated people out of the ballroom. Nobody seemed keen on going out into the cold. Those who had rooms at the mansion hardly understood where they were any longer. Charlotte made another announcement over the speaker system to say that keys were located at the front desk in the foyer for those who hadn't checked into their rooms yet. This was answered with another howl, a series of jeers, and then the crash of a champagne glass against the floor.

Great.

Tommy, Everett, and Zach seemed to create a superhero team after that. Charlotte watched them in awe as they marched through the tables, dropped down to demand action from various members of the party, and then even occasionally helped them into their coats or jackets with words of encouragement, like, "Be safe out there! See you tomorrow!" When Charlotte heard Tommy say words like that, he grunted at her and said, "Listen. I'm a moody SOB, but there's no way I want to give your party a bad rep."

This warmed her heart more than almost anything else. She had never really bonded with Lola's newfound beau, the handsome Tommy Gasbarro, but she now totally approved of him. She made a mental note to tell Lola. Finally, she had found somebody to love and worthy of her grandness.

Rachel, too, found her way with the kick-out crew. Charlotte watched as Rachel placed a hand on an unsteady actress, who stood in six-inch heels and blubbered drunkenly to herself.

"It's okay! Your limo is just outside," Rachel said, sounding every bit like a twenty-one-year-old. "Remember? I called your driver?"

"Rachel! You're such a darling," the actress returned in a British accent.

She was good. Charlotte couldn't tell if she was actually British or not.

"You'll call me when you come to London, won't you, Rachel?" the actress cried as Rachel walked her toward the door.

"Yes. You're going to show me your favorite fish and chips shop," Rachel said. Her voice was flat and patient.

"You're going to love it. Oh, Rachel, why wasn't I as wise as you when I was your age?"

Charlotte giggled inwardly. When Rachel turned back, having delivered the actress to her limo, she rolled her eyes.

"Don't let me ever drink alcohol," Rachel said. "It turns people stupid."

"You might want to feel a little stupid sometimes," Charlotte said, rubbing her daughter's back.

"I do not understand that," Rachel said, bug-eyed. "But I'll take your word for it."

Finally, after what seemed like an hour or more, the only people who remained in the ballroom were: Zach, Christine, Lola, Tommy, Charlotte, Claire, Rachel, and Everett. Zach was still hot-headed from earlier. He stomped over to the bar and poured himself two fingers of whiskey. Nobody spoke for a long time.

"Well," Tommy said, looking on the verge of spitting. "Looks like that's it, then. We lived through night one."

Charlotte burst forward. "I can't thank you guys enough. I know that was hell."

"It was. But it was also hilarious," Zach said, already buttering himself up with the whiskey.

"Really?" Charlotte asked.

Zach took a sip, furrowed his brow, then said, "No. But I'll remember it, I guess. That's something."

"What about clean-up?" Lola asked.

"We aren't using this space tomorrow," Charlotte said. "So it'll get it cleaned in the morning while we're setting up ball-room number two."

"So those crazy kids are really going to go through with it?" Zach asked.

"Don't jinx it," Christine said. She walked toward him, wrapped her arm around him, and placed a kiss on his cheek.

"He looks like he's on the verge of walking right out," Tommy said.

Lola swatted his bicep and gave him an ominous look. He shrugged and said, "What?"

"I don't care how long they stay married. I just need this entire event to fall through without a hitch," Charlotte said. "If they divorce in a year? I'll hardly bat an eye. But we need them to walk down that aisle tomorrow, or else I've failed."

Everyone fell silent. After a little while, Christine suggested that they all head home to get some much-needed rest. Charlotte stared at her shoes, embarrassed. Had she made everyone mad? Uncomfortable? Of course she had. It hadn't been necessary. She supposed she just didn't have total control over her own emotions just then.

Suddenly, Everett appeared beside her. She knew it first by the musk of his smell, mixed with his cologne. Something inside of her swirled with anxiety, and she felt her heart beat faster. Was that excitement? Attraction? She wasn't sure because these new feelings were so strange to her.

"I just called myself a taxi," he told her under his breath while the others spoke. "I wondered if you and Rachel wanted to leave with me. You've had one hell of a night."

Charlotte turned her eyes toward his cobalt blue ones. Her stomach stirred with exhaustion, but she felt her lips creak up into a smile. "Are you sure?" she breathed.

"Of course. It's just across the island. If you think you can handle a taxi ride with me after the night, you've had..."

"Of course," she insisted. "I appreciate it. I'll let Rachel know we're about to go."

Just before the taxi arrived, Charlotte grabbed a bottle of whiskey from the open bar and stuffed it in her bag. It wasn't the high-end stuff, more the medium-variety—something these high-rollers wouldn't remember. In the midst of a multi-million-dollar wedding, Charlotte supposed one bottle of whiskey back at her place wouldn't hurt.

She then hugged her family members—first Lola and Christine, of course, then Tommy, then Zach, then Claire, who she found in another heap of flowers in the parlor, brimming with tears.

"You should go home," she told Claire, placing her hand on her sister's tender cheek. "I promise. Everything will be brighter in the morning."

"The very early morning," Claire corrected. "I need to fix this bouquet before that lady walks down the aisle."

Charlotte chortled. "That *lady*. You just called Ursula Pennington *that lady*."

Claire burst into laughter. "I know. She would hate it, wouldn't she?"

"So much. I love it, though," Charlotte affirmed.

Charlotte, Rachel, and Everett stood out on the snow-capped curb, waiting for the taxi. Above them, the stars twinkled daintily, as though they had secrets of their own. Rachel lifted her chin toward the black night sky and said, "They're much more beautiful in winter, aren't they?"

"I always thought so," Charlotte replied. "But I never thought anyone else did."

"They're beautiful here," Everett said. "I've never been here in the summertime. But I can't imagine anything better than this."

"You should come back in the summer," Rachel said brightly. "It's really magical. Swimming and boating and... Well, Mom doesn't like to swim that much."

"Really?" Everett said. He cast her a funny smile. "Surrounded by water, and you hate it?"

"I don't hate it," Charlotte said, sniffing. "I just find it beautiful to look at. I don't necessarily need to be in it."

Everett and Rachel both shrugged.

"Suit yourself," Everett said.

When the taxi pulled up, the three of them piled in: Rachel in the center of the back, Charlotte on the left, and Everett on the right. Charlotte couldn't help but wonder: did the driver think they were a family? What did that make her feel? Was it a betrayal to Jason?

Should I somehow express the fact that Everett is nothing to me? Just a new friend?

But how could I say that without totally killing this mood between Everett and I?

Focus. It doesn't matter.

Nobody else is thinking about this except you.

"We've sure got a lot of snow this year," the taxi driver said suddenly.

"Sure do!" both Charlotte and Everett answered at once.

Both of them sounded strange, so strange that they turned their eyes toward one another and burst into laughter.

Okay. She was overreacting, probably.

They were just friends.

Good friends.

She couldn't just mess that up because she was a sad, lonely widow, aching for some kind of recognition in the world.

Could she even accept love if it was handed to her?

She wasn't sure.

Chapter Seventeen

When tensions rose between Everett and Charlotte, Everett found it funny that one of the two of them would burst into laughter—as though both of them knew how middle-school-silly any sort of affection was. Sure, maybe if he was twelve, he would have said, *I have a crazy crush on Charlotte Hamner.* But he wasn't twelve, and he was there on Martha's Vineyard to do a job, sell some photographs, then head back to LA to spend it on some overpriced rent (although decently priced for the neighborhood he lived in!), cocktails, and dates with models who didn't have any feelings.

He tried to burn these thoughts into his mind.

But they really didn't stick.

When the taxi reached Charlotte's house, he turned his eyes toward hers and tried to drum up the strength to say good-night. Instead, he heard the first real music of the night when she said, "Why don't you come in for a bit? There's a lot to unpack from tonight. I'm exhausted, but I don't want to forget a minute."

Everett reached forward to pay the driver before Charlotte could. She half-heartedly swatted his hand away, then said, "Whatever. I'll get it next time," as though there would be a whole series of next-times together in the back of a taxi.

It was enough to make Everett's heart surge with hope.

He wasn't sure what to do with that hope.

He crunched through the snow behind Rachel and Charlotte. A quick glance at his phone told him that it was just after one in the morning. Still, his head buzzed with adrenaline. It could have been the middle of the day.

Charlotte drew open the door to allow him to enter. Inside was a little foyer with red tile, a mudroom off to the side, a kitchen, a living area, two bedrooms, and a bathroom. Everything was decorated warmly, comfortably—completely unlike the swanky party they had just attended.

"Your taste is nothing like Ursula Pennington's," Everett said with a laugh as he removed his shoes slowly and placed them in the mudroom.

"What can I say? Friends tell me my number one attribute is that I'm not a millionaire," Charlotte said with a funny laugh.

Rachel yawned. She looked on the verge of collapse. "I'm going to go take a shower and get into bed," she said. "I'll see you in the morning?"

She spoke pointedly only at her mother. Everett seethed with sudden panic. He realized that he had just put himself in an awkward position, forcing himself into their home after one in the morning. Probably, this made Rachel uncomfortable?

But as she turned down the little hallway, she called back, "Good night, Everett."

"Good night, Rachel," he returned.

In the silence that filled the space between them, Charlotte performed a similar routine to Rachel. "I'd like to get out of these clothes if you don't mind."

"Sure. I'll be out here."

"I'll boil some water. Make some hot cocoa with..." Charlotte yanked open a swankier bottle of whiskey, one she had clearly taken from the rehearsal dinner.

"You little thief," Everett said, grinning from ear to ear.

Charlotte laughed and disappeared for a moment. As Everett sat there alone, he glanced around the living area—over the TV, on the refrigerator, toward the foyer, where Charlotte, Rachel, and another man lurked in nearly every single photo.

Right. Trevor had said something about a disaster.

Here he sat, in the epicenter of that disaster.

Compared to all that, he was nothing.

The thought didn't make him feel bad, exactly. It wasn't like he had known the guy or known the circumstances. Still, he didn't want to be any reminder of that tragedy: another big man in the house, mentally *into* Charlotte in a way he couldn't really describe.

He had to be on his best behavior.

He didn't want to push any buttons.

Which probably meant he couldn't remove any.

Not that he'd gotten out of the taxi with her to do that!

Now, he was safely stuck in his head. He shook it violently and again studied the photos. The guy in them hadn't died that long ago, clearly, since Rachel wasn't so young in many of them. What had happened? Car accident? Murder? No. That was ridiculous. People didn't just get murdered.

"Are you okay?" Charlotte appeared in a light pink robe. She had removed a little bit of her makeup, and her hair still billowed around her beautifully.

"Yeah! Just thinking about tonight," Everett lied.

"It was wild, wasn't it?" Charlotte said. She walked to the stove, poured two glasses of boiling water, added hot cocoa, then poured what looked to be two fingers of whiskey.

"Somebody is looking to party," Everett said, teasing her.

Charlotte laughed—thank goodness, since the second he'd said it, he'd regretted it.

"Those people make me insane," she said. "I don't know. Do you think they've always been rich? Never had anyone to answer to? I feel like most of them looked at me and thought, 'Yes. I can take advantage of her because she's only half the person I am.' It makes my stomach hurt. Oh, but that's been a facet of growing up on Martha's Vineyard, I guess. When summer happens, the big politicians and celebrities come through, and you're nothing to them."

"I guess it's kind of similar in LA," Everett said, agreeing with her.

"Oh, of course," she said. "I keep forgetting. You're used to all these celebrities and their obsession with Instagram and all that. I feel like I'm on the outside."

"I'm not saying that I like that they're like that," Everett said with a laugh. "Only that's them. For better or for worse."

"For better or for worse. Nice use of the wedding vows," Charlotte said.

"I thought you'd like that," Everett replied.

This time, her cheeks turned bright pink. Clearly, he had gone too far again—or maybe just gotten too flirtatious? Where was the line? He didn't know!

"I really appreciate what you did earlier when Ursula was yelling at me," Charlotte said. "I didn't know how to get her to stop yelling. It was just her stream of consciousness at that point."

"She can't taint her image like that," Everett said. "It would have ruined her."

"Paul Thomas Anderson would not have called her up again, that's for sure," Charlotte stated.

They sipped their hot chocolate whiskey drinks. Everett blinked forward but accidentally caught sight of another of those family photos. He had no idea what to say next. Maybe he had run out of topics forever. Maybe he'd never said anything interesting at all.

"Why did you get involved with wedding planning?" he suddenly asked.

This was a good start, wasn't it? A way to actually get to know her?

"That's a good question," she said. She sipped her drink again and thought for a moment. "I guess my main answer is, I always want to see people on their happiest days, as ironic as that sounds after what we just saw."

"Their happiest days," Everett breathed.

"Does that sound crazy?" Charlotte asked. She knocked her head back against the couch cushion and blinked up toward the ceiling.

"Not at all," Everett affirmed. "I can even understand it. Although I do think it's rare to see that, even on the wedding day itself."

Charlotte arched her brow and turned her gaze toward his. "Why do you say that?"

"Well, beyond what we just saw—which is obviously a crazy outlier, I feel that mostly, I see a lot of fake happiness on wedding days," he said. "People who are overly willing to put on loads of makeup and feign smile after smile until the clock strikes twelve. And it's funny, you know? Sometimes, I'll take photos where I think, wow, these people. They look really happy here. And they almost never actually buy the photos of actual happiness. Fake happiness sells better. Maybe it's because that's the happiness we see reflected back in advertisements. It's the happiness we're told to want, so it's the happiness we buy."

Charlotte nodded somberly. "That makes sense."

Everett felt as though he had killed the mood. He looked at his half-drunk whiskey and cocoa and considered a way out of the room.

But instead, Charlotte spoke.

"Have you ever been married? I just realized. I barely know anything about you."

Everett laughed. "That's funny, isn't it? We've gone to war, basically, but we don't know anything about the other."

"And so, I ask..."

"Right. No. I've never been married. This actually came up with your cousins at the bar. They said they've never been married, either," Everett said.

"True. But look at them. They're well on their way. Lola's thirty-nine years old, and I've never seen her more in love than she is with Tommy. Christine has had a mountain of boyfriends, but now, at forty-one, she seems ready to settle with Zach."

"I would marry him for his cooking alone," Everett joked.

"Ha. Maybe I'll steal him away," Charlotte teased.

"But really. I never thought marriage was worth my time since I wanted so many things along the way," Everett explained. "I wanted to travel. I wanted to spend a year in Asia. I wanted to build my photography career. I wanted..." He paused. All the words he said seemed like stories that belonged to someone else's life. "Anyway, nothing ever really worked out the way I planned."

"Was there anyone along the way? Anyone you might have married? If you could just turn back the clock?"

Everett shook his head. "It's sad to say, but I really never allowed myself to feel that way for anyone. I kept myself guarded. And now... Well. I'm forty-four. Single."

"And ready to mingle," Charlotte said, her voice lilting, joking.

"Something like that," Everett said.

Now. Kiss her now. It's obvious she wants it. Her eyes are glittering; she's even tilted her face toward yours.

This is so obvious.

Kiss her.

But he couldn't. He couldn't do it there, in front of all these photographs of this other man. Not without knowing what had happened. Not without understanding her better.

He cared for her too much.

He had only known her a day, for God's sake.

How stupid of him.

Suddenly, the spell was broken. Charlotte's lips erupted with a yawn. When the yawn broke, she laughed and sipped the rest of her drink.

"My gosh. I'm exhausted. Do you mind if I head to bed? Do you want to head back to the Inn?"

"I might just collapse here if you don't mind," Everett said. His eyelashes fluttered across his cheeks for a moment until he summoned the strength to yank them back up.

"Of course. I'll grab you a blanket."

Everett watched in awe as Charlotte splayed a thick quilt over him. "Are you comfortable enough?" she asked him, as though this was her greatest concern in the world.

It had been a long time since Everett had been someone's greatest concern in the world.

"It's perfect. Thank you," he replied.

Minutes or even seconds later, Everett was cast into darkness. He slept like a little kid after a long day of play. He only knew that when he woke up, he would find a way to help Charlotte through the rest of the weekend. And he knew it wouldn't be easy.

Chapter Eighteen

Charlotte stood at the barrier between the hallway and her living area at five-thirty in the morning, wide awake and bright-eyed, staring at the still-sleeping form of one Everett Rainey, a man she had literally just met.

What had she done?

She remembered the night, of course—at least, most of it. She remembered wanting to take care of him, to make him a bit of cocoa (and whiskey, if memory served her correctly), and to ask him about his thoughts.

Did she remember asking him to stay over? Why had he just slept on the couch?

Had she tried to kiss him or something?

That wasn't really like her. After all, it had taken her years to kiss a boy for the first time. That boy had been Jason, who had later become her husband.

Shoot. She was the most inexperienced person on the planet.

And here she was, before one of the more experienced people she'd probably ever met.

Was she falling for him?

Would she really allow herself to do that?

Surely, she was more responsible than that.

Oh, but why did she care so much? Why did he seem to care so much? When Ursula had berated her the night before, Charlotte had thought there was no way out, that she would have to endure the depths of all that pain and torment until Ursula got bored of it.

And then, there he had been—her knight in shining armor.

Charlotte had a number of people to call and things to take care of that morning. She tried to redirect her thoughts to include these elements only. Any sort of romance brewing between her and the photographer would have to wait for another day. Assuredly, that other day would come, and he would be long gone.

Better to keep herself safe from emotion.

Charlotte brewed a pot of coffee as quietly as she could. Now that he was there, fast asleep, in all of his clothes (should she have offered him something? No. That "something" would have belonged to Jason, and that felt even more wrong than everything else)—she might as well allow him to sleep.

Just as she poured herself a big cup of black coffee, Rachel appeared beside her. Charlotte nearly leaped out of her robe.

"Hey, honey," she said, trying to stifle her tremendous fear. "Sorry. I didn't know you were awake."

Rachel tilted her head toward Everett. "He slept over," she whispered.

"I guess so. He must have passed out before heading back to the Inn."

Rachel gave her a look that meant, *If that's what you want me to believe, I'll believe it. I guess.*

"Seriously," Charlotte said, giving her daughter a wide-eyed stare.

Rachel grabbed the box of Pop-Tarts from the top of the

fridge and yanked open the silver package. She took a small nibble from the top of a brown sugar cinnamon, then chewed contemplatively.

"What are you thinking?" Charlotte breathed.

"I was just wondering if this might become a thing."

"What kind of a thing?"

"Like, are you going to start dating again?" Rachel's eyes bore into Charlotte's.

Charlotte grabbed the silver package, yanked out the other Pop-Tart, and took her own bite. "No," she said and took another bite before continuing. "Your father has only been gone a little over a year. I know that. You know that. It's not like we can just walk away from that life so easily. Maybe I'll never be ready to. I don't know."

Rachel arched her brow. "Apparently, Aunt Claire is worried that you'll never find anyone."

"Oh my God. Of course she is. But I have you, don't I?"

Rachel grumbled. "For now. But Mom, I'm fourteen. What if I want to go to college off the island? And what if I get a job in New York City, like Christine, or Boston, like Lola? And what if I move to Paris or go to Rome or..."

Charlotte stretched her palm out between them and shook it. "You're getting ahead of yourself, don't you think?"

Rachel shrugged. "I just think maybe we shouldn't focus on the past so much. That's all."

This was the wrong time to have this conversation. Charlotte felt that in every part of herself, in the way her throat constricted and the way her heart lurched into her stomach. After all, the first man she had ever been attracted to outside of Jason Hamner currently slept on their couch, only about six feet away.

Still, a small, horrible kernel of her heart told her that her daughter was right.

Maybe it was stupid to wait.

Maybe Jason wanted her to move on.

Charlotte tore off another piece of Pop Tart and grumbled, "Why do you keep doing this?"

"Doing what?" Rachel demanded.

"Proving how old you are? It's making me feel silly. You're going to have to be my boss soon," Charlotte said.

Suddenly, Everett erupted from the couch—so fast that the quilt fell off his legs and he yelped with fear.

Immediately, both Charlotte and Rachel burst into laughter. Everett turned his wide eyes toward them, clearly coming out of some kind of nightmare. He looked at them like he had never seen them before in his life. If Charlotte hadn't been more sensible, she might have thought he was possessed.

"My gosh," he said suddenly. He rubbed his cheeks, coming out of his panic. "I had no idea where I was."

"We figured as much," Rachel said, still giggling. "You looked like you were getting chased out of your dream by monsters."

"Ha. It was kind of like that, actually," Everett said. "Actually, I usually do that when I'm at someone else's place. I wake up like a crazy person. I'm sorry about that."

Rachel shrugged. "Thanks for the comedy routine. Want a Pop-Tart?" She grabbed another silver package and passed it to him.

He took it and thanked her. "I don't think I've had one of these in like twenty years," he replied, looking at the package in his hand.

"As you shouldn't," Charlotte said. "They'll rot every single part of your body."

"Except for your heart," Everett said teasingly.

There: he had done it again. He had tugged at something inside of Charlotte's mind, something that told her, *This guy is different. This guy has the potential to be something more.*

Shoot.

Rachel and Charlotte watched as Everett struggled with the silver packaging. Finally, impatient, Rachel grabbed the package and yanked it off, passing a full pastry to him.

"Thanks. I guess it's too early for me to do anything," he said with a laugh.

Charlotte poured him a cup of coffee. He thanked her and perched at the edge of the stool near the side of the kitchen. His dark brown curls shook around his ears and into his eyes. It was the ultimate bedhead.

He looked adorable, though.

"What are your plans this morning?" Charlotte asked brightly. Outside, the sun brimmed over the horizon line and cast the snow in its first glittering light.

"Well, I guess I had better go back to the Inn, shower, and change out of these clothes," Everett said. "Seems like a pretty good place to begin."

"Makes sense," Charlotte said.

"And then I guess I plan to meet you guys back at the mansion around, what, noon?"

"We plan to start decorating around then, so that's perfect," Charlotte affirmed.

"You gonna put me to work?" he asked, chuckling.

"Absolutely. It'll be like day one, but ten times better. We're pulling out all the stops. Which reminds me..." Charlotte furrowed her brow, remembering Claire. "Claire needs our help this morning, probably as soon as we can get to the flower shop. Rachel?"

"I'm on it!" Rachel cried. She finished the rest of her Pop-Tart, spun on her heel, and hustled back toward the bathroom. In just a few seconds, they heard the sound of the shower.

"Guess that's my cue," Everett said. He saluted her with the Pop-Tart and said, "Thanks for breakfast."

"Breakfast of champions, right?" Charlotte said. She couldn't help but grin to herself.

"That's what I always say."

Charlotte and Rachel dragged themselves out of the house around forty-five minutes later and marched the rest of the way to Claire's flower shop. When they creaked open the door, they heard Claire's voice toward the back. They burst forward and found her surrounded in another heap of flowers, her cheeks blotchy.

"I can't find the lily of the valley," she said. "I thought I had it. I..."

"It's over here, Mom!" Abby called from the far end of the room, where she was actually hidden by another few boxes of flowers.

"It's like heaven in here," Charlotte said.

"I don't know if that's how I would put it," Claire said.

"What can we do?" Charlotte demanded.

Claire put the girls to work over the next few hours, arranging the boutonniere and the bouquets carefully. "I've already sent a few vans of flowers over to the mansion itself. The staff should be halfway through decorating by now," Claire affirmed.

"I think I want to get over there to check it out," Charlotte said. "I'm getting nervous and want to make sure the ballroom is set up, not to mention the dining hall."

"That dining hall is immaculate," Claire said, clucking her tongue. "I don't think I'd seen it before yesterday when we started to set up."

"It is, isn't it? Fit for a princess like Ursula."

"What are you talking about? Ursula is a queen," Claire said, rolling her eyes.

"Maybe she'll be better behaved today," Rachel said doubtfully.

"Maybe," Charlotte said.

Claire gave her a funny look as Abby, Rachel, and Gail took a load of flowers out to the van.

"What's been going on with you and that photographer, by the way?" she asked.

Charlotte shook her head. "What are you talking about?"

"You know. He seems to watch out for you. He's always looking for you. I don't know. People have been talking."

"There's always gossip going around this family, isn't there?" Charlotte said. "But no. Sorry to disappoint. I'm just glad to have a rational photographer in the mix. Plus, he works for *Wedding Today*, which means there's a chance we could work together in the future."

"Oh. So, you're networking," Claire said, arching an eyebrow at her sister.

"I can hear from your tone that you're teasing me, and I want you to know that I don't appreciate it," Charlotte retorted with her hands on her hips.

As Abby, Gail, and Rachel returned from outside, Abby called out, "Apparently, that hot photographer slept at Rachel's house last night!"

Claire's jaw dropped. "Charlotte!"

"He slept on the couch!" Charlotte blared. "It was cold out, and it just kind of happened."

But there was no getting that glint out of Claire's eyes. Charlotte grumbled to herself and gave Rachel a slightly dirty look. "Thanks for getting me in trouble," she muttered as she walked past. "Claire won't let me live this one down."

* * *

When they arrived at the mansion, they parked the van along the far side, closer to the Nantucket Sound. Charlotte crunched out across the snow and gazed out across the waters. They seemed darker, more secretive, and somehow more sinister than they normally did. Sometimes, she had a hard time looking out over them, as her mind always went there.

That storm, creeping in, taking over Jason's boat...

She shook her long locks and turned around to spot Lola driving up with Christine and Zach in tow. The next car delivered Audrey, Amanda, and Susan. Charlotte waved hello and pointed toward the double-wide and two-story-tall doors, which Claire and the girls had already propped open.

"Just head that way. Claire will put you to work," she said.

At that moment, a taxi pulled up. A dark boot whipped out and onto the snowy pavement below. Next came that voice: gritty and so masculine, it sent chills up and down her spine.

"Hey there," Everett said after he had paid. As the taxi skidded out of the parking lot, he lifted his camera and said, "Do you mind? You look great with the water backdrop. The sun's hitting your hair just perfectly."

Charlotte rolled her eyes. "Don't waste any of your camera space on me. I'm the wedding planner. I get paid to be as invisible as possible."

"Come on. This is the last day of your anonymity," Everett argued. "After this, your phone is going to ring off the hook."

Charlotte allowed him to snap one, two, and then three photos when she finally threw up her hands and said, "Enough! I have to go help my decorators. And if I'm not mistaken, I promised you a few jobs as well."

"I'm here to serve," Everett said. "I spotted a few other photographers in Oak Bluffs, by the way. Tabloid people, probably coming to stand outside the mansion and take photos as people come in beforehand."

"Great," Charlotte said sarcastically. "Even more drama to deal with."

"In twenty-four hours, this will all be over."

"Yeah. Or the mansion will be on fire, Ursula will want my head, and the newsstands will all read, 'Infamous Wedding Planner on the Run,'" Charlotte said.

"Wherever you end up, send me a secret letter, so I know," Everett said.

"You mean like in *The Shawshank Redemption*?" Charlotte asked.

"Exactly. Glad you got it."

Charlotte half-skipped into the mansion to find her incredible crew hard at work on the decorations. The place looked astounding, almost exactly the way she had pictured it, with more than fifteen Christmas trees decorated with gorgeous hanging bulbs made of crystal, chandeliers that reflected the beautiful sunlight that streamed in from the east, and long, thin tables reminiscent of long-ago balls held at that very mansion. As she gazed out at her dearest family members, Rachel rose up on a ladder and placed a perfect crystal bulb near the top of the largest Christmas tree. She inspected it, her hands on her hips, pleased.

Everything was suddenly falling into place.

Which meant, of course, that it was time for the phone to ring with news of disaster.

Chapter Nineteen

"Charlotte? Charlotte, is that you?"

Charlotte immediately recognized the frantic voice of Ursula's mother, who she had spoken to only briefly the day before but many times over the previous weeks.

"Yes, of course. What's wrong?" Her heart pattered wildly in her throat.

"Charlotte, you need to get up here. We have a little bit of a situation."

"Are you in Ursula's suite?" Charlotte asked.

"No. Um." Wind crackled and whipped across the phone on the other end, proof that they were outside somewhere. "I'm not sure where we are, to be honest with you. She just burst outside and started to run."

Ugh.

"Okay. Can you describe your surroundings, maybe?"

"It's this long, skinny strip of sand," Mrs. Pennington continued. "I don't know. I see a sign, but it's all covered with snow."

"Joseph Sylvia. Of course. I'll be there as soon as I can," Charlotte said.

Charlotte pressed her phone to her chest and blinked up into the lovely eyes of Everett Rainey.

"You look like something's wrong," he told her.

"Something seems to always be wrong with this wedding," she replied. She suddenly erupted with a hiccup and felt so embarrassed. She placed her hand over her mouth abruptly and grimaced. "I'm so sorry. I think the stress is just..." She hiccupped again.

Everett's smile was infectious. "Let me guess. You have to go find Ursula?"

Charlotte nodded with her hand still pressed over her mouth. Her entire body jumped again with another hiccup. "But I can't go like this," she said, her voice quivering through her fingers. "Not with the hiccups. Ugh! Today started out so well!"

"Just breathe deeply," Everett told her. "In for four counts, out for four counts. You're just stressed. I used to get the hiccups all the time before piano competitions."

Charlotte let her hand drop and followed Everett's guidance: in for four, out for four. Slowly, she walked toward the exit, totally focused on her breath and her footwork. By the time she grabbed her coat from the coat room, she felt the hiccups dissipate.

"That actually worked..." she said to Everett, who had followed her with his camera.

"I told you."

"Wait. You play the piano? Never mind. I'd like to ask you more about this, but right now..."

"Ursula calls," Everett affirmed.

Gumdrop-sized snowflakes floated down from the sky. Charlotte gripped the top of her skirt to allow her legs to stretch out before her, limber and quick. Everett hustled beside her.

The air felt sharp in her throat, yet so clear. It was like drinking ice water.

When they reached the Joseph Sylvia State Beach, they stopped short at the sight before them.

Near the waves, wearing only her stark white and barely-there wedding dress, stood Ursula.

The picture itself was one of the most beautiful images Charlotte had ever seen.

The wind whipped Ursula's blond locks around and tore at the bottom of her lacey wedding dress, curving it across the sand. Her hands lifted her skirts slightly at the front to allow her toes to tip into the very first of the rushing waves. As the chilly water rushed toward her ankles, Ursula's bright red lips curved into a smile.

"She looks like she has totally lost it," Charlotte breathed, placing a hand on her forehead. How would she get Ursula back into the mansion?

Everett snapped several photos. Charlotte couldn't blame him. The sight was extraordinary. Someone had to record it.

Ursula's mother was several feet behind her daughter, calling her name. The sound of it was tremendously horrible, strained, and sad.

"Ursula, baby, come back over here. Let's talk about it! Come now. It's so chilly out here. You're going to catch a cold."

Charlotte hustled the rest of the way to Ursula's mother, careful not to get too close to the icy water or Ursula herself. When she reached Mrs. Pennington, the woman gave her a look of incredulity, like, *Who are you?*

"Mrs. Pennington. I came as quickly as I could."

"Oh. Yes. Of course." Mrs. Pennington's eyes filled with tears. "She's a tiny bit drunk, I'm afraid, and having second thoughts."

Charlotte's heart surged with fear. "Second thoughts are

totally normal. I see this all the time with young brides on their wedding day."

In actuality, Charlotte had only seen one bride with second thoughts—and that bride hadn't gotten drunk and tried to walk into the ocean at the end of November.

But it was better to lie right now.

"Really?" Mrs. Pennington asked.

"Of course."

Charlotte scrunched her nose and tip-toed through the sand toward Ursula. When she reached her, a wave rushed up and completely drenched her boot. The chill shot through her feet and her calves. Her fingers were already turning blue.

"Ursula?" Charlotte said. Her voice hardly rang out through the wind.

Ursula slowly turned her face toward Charlotte. The motion was strangely robotic, and her eyes were glassy, proof of her drunkenness.

Still, her eyeliner was killer.

She was every bit the classic movie star the world wanted her to be. Just a little bit more messed up.

"Ursula, what are you doing out here?" Charlotte asked softly.

Ursula staggered a bit. Charlotte was ready to throw herself forward, if only to save that gorgeous wedding dress from being drenched in the waves.

"I don't think I really love him," Ursula stated. She bit hard on her lower lip and let a few tears fall.

"Okay. That's okay. Um. Why don't we go inside and talk about it a little bit more?"

"I just think I'm doing it because my agent said the public wanted to watch me grow up," she continued. "I got my first Oscar when I was twenty-four years old. And now, I'm nearing thirty, and I'm like—what's next? So I guess this is next?"

"It doesn't have to be next if you don't want it to be." Charlotte willed the girl to get cold enough to take this introspective conversation indoors.

"But then what? I go in there and tell Orion that this is all a farce? And really—I mean, if we're getting down to the actual facts here, I don't believe that he didn't cheat on me, either on his bachelor week, or after an away game, or..."

"You don't know that for sure," Charlotte argued, trying to knock some sense into her.

Ursula's lower lip bubbled. She dropped her chin toward her chest, totally defeated. Charlotte reached forward, grabbed her elbow—which was as cold as steel in winter—and said, "Let's get you inside, okay? I make the best hot cocoa known to man. Maybe I can make you some."

Surprisingly, the idea of hot cocoa was the thing that finally got acclaimed actress Ursula Pennington away from the hungry waves and back inside. When they arrived back at the mansion, they entered the wing nearest to Ursula's suite. Ursula walked like a stunted model, her legs hardly bending at the knee. Charlotte and Mrs. Pennington hovered behind her. When Charlotte turned back to close the door of the wing, she found Everett there. She had completely forgotten about him in all the chaos.

"What's up?" he asked, his beautiful eyes wide.

Charlotte heaved a sigh and spoke under her breath. "Apparently, Ursula is having second thoughts."

"Oh, no."

"I know."

"You've gone through all this just so she can cancel last-minute?"

"I know. I know. My head might spin off my neck," Charlotte said, biting her lower lip as she felt her anxiety build.

"Well. Huh. Okay." Everett scratched under his chin. "Maybe I can go talk to him."

"To whom?"

"Orion."

Charlotte shrugged. "I'm willing to try anything to get these two down the aisle. Ursula is convinced Orion cheated on her. Maybe if you can get him to say he didn't?"

Everett considered this. "Do you think it's immoral to try to force two people we don't know to marry each other for the sake of our own personal gain?"

Charlotte laughed. The words were so outrageous. The whole thing was, actually. "We can't force them to do anything. Let's just see where the wind takes us today."

At this, Everett lifted his camera and took another shot of Charlotte, standing there in the doorway. He inspected the photo on the little screen and laughed to himself.

"What's so funny? Do I look like I'm having the worst day of my life?"

Everett's blue eyes found hers again. "No. You look beautiful."

With that, Everett turned and marched toward the other wing, which led toward Orion's suite. Charlotte watched as the snow fluttered down around them. This was the strangest day.

Chapter Twenty

Everett arrived outside Orion's suite a few minutes later. His heart hummed in his throat; his skin was spiky with a chill, and his mind buzzed with memory of Charlotte. He couldn't remember the last time a woman had looked at him like that. Like he, himself, owned the world and could give it to her.

A split second after Everett knocked on the door, one of Orion's seven-foot-tall teammates ripped it open and looked at him with a sour expression.

"Can I help you?" His eyes scanned down toward Everett's camera. "No photos."

"Oh, no. I'm actually here because of Ursula," Everett explained. "I need to speak to Orion."

"Orion doesn't want to be spoken to," the teammate boomed.

"I understand that. But it's important." Everett caught sight of Orion at the far end of the suite. He was hunched forward, his elbows on his knees, a glass of something that looked an awful lot like whiskey in his hand. "I know Ursula tried to call off the wedding. I think there's a way we can save it."

The silence stretched between all of them. Another teammate whispered something in Orion's ear. Finally, Orion grunted and said, "Let the photographer in."

The first teammate shut the door closed immediately after Everett stepped inside, nearly clipping it against the back of his boots. The mood in the suite was ominous. Orion himself looked as though he had been hit by a truck. He sipped more of his whiskey and gestured toward the chair in front of him.

"You said you think you can save my wedding? Sit down and tell me how," he ordered. His words were heavy with sarcasm, and his eyes said, *You think you, of all people, have the answers? Yeah. Right.*

"Good afternoon, Orion," Everett said as he sat down. "I was just downstairs with your fiancé. She really is upset about all of this."

Orion grunted and lifted his phone. "She just sent me a load of gibberish telling me the wedding is off. I guess that's all I need to know. I mean, there's a lot the public doesn't understand about little-miss-perfect Ursula Pennington."

Little Miss Perfect? Ha.

"I'm sure that's true," Everett agreed, keeping his voice flat and diplomatic. "I'm sure the world will never really understand your relationship."

"No way. It's so complicated. We're different, Ursula and me, but we're also the same in so many ways. It's why I don't even know if I want to fight her on this decision. If she wants out, she wants out. I have to let her fly."

Orion knocked back the rest of his whiskey and then shuddered. A tear fell from the corner of his left eye. "I just don't know what I'm going to do without her, you know? We've been together for almost two years. It feels like a lifetime."

Everett imagined saying this to Charlotte later. *The kid*

140

thinks two years together is a lifetime. Wait till he figures out what a lifetime actually means!

"I understand that," Everett said, nodding. "Is there any chance—just off-hand—that you might have, I don't know, cheated on her?"

Orion's eyes nearly popped out of his head. "What?"

"I mean, on your bachelor weekend. Ursula seems to think something might have happened. Maybe this is part of the reason she's getting cold feet?"

Orion burst up from his chair and marched his seven-foot-tall body over to the drink table. As he poured another glass of whiskey for himself, he barked at his friend near the window. "Baxter. Did anything happen in Malibu? Anything I might have done or said?"

"No way, man. You told us all how much you loved Ursula. Way too many times, actually," Baxter said. His voice was bored, and his eyes didn't leave his phone as he said it. But it was proof enough for Orion.

"See? I swear, that girl drives me crazy, but I want to marry her. Still, I'm not an idiot enough to run after her. If she wants to end it, then it's over. Here we are, in the middle of literally nowhere." He stretched his hand out toward the snow-capped Martha's Vineyard out the window. "And the girl of my dreams tells me she never wants to see me again. I'm man enough to admit that there's no going back."

Everett tilted his head. He had to find a way to butter this guy up. Obviously, he and Charlotte had these two crazy, ego-driven celebrities in front of them, and they had to convince them both to do what they actually *wanted to do—get married* —to ensure that their careers could continue to flourish.

It shouldn't have been this hard.

"Do you believe in second chances?" Everett asked spontaneously.

Orion looked as though he had never been asked a question

like that before. He took several moments to contemplate his answer.

"I think I do," he said finally. "But only if the person is really perfect for you. Only if you're okay with making the same mistakes, over and over again."

"But what if you don't make those mistakes? It's a little like playing a video game, right? You play the first round, and then you die somehow. The next time you play, you know to avoid that pitfall, and you keep going. You find a new kingdom or a better route or..." Everett shrugged.

Orion seemed in tune with this idea. "That's such a good analogy."

"Agreed," his friend by the window called out, his eyes still on his phone.

"Have you ever fought for anything as hard as that?" Orion asked Everett.

Everett hadn't expected the big-time sports star to ask him a question in return.

"Honestly? No," Everett stated.

"I see. So you're spouting a lot of logic that you don't know anything about," Orion said.

Everett laughed. "I guess I am."

"Then why should I believe you?"

"I don't know. Maybe you shouldn't," Everett said, shrugging his shoulders before he continued. "I do think that, if I ever found something worthy enough to fight for, I would do all I could to keep it. At least, I have to believe that about myself."

Orion considered this. "Do you think I'll regret marrying her?"

"I think you'll regret never knowing what would happen after you walked down the aisle and said those vows," Everett said.

Orion looked confused. He poured a second glass of whiskey and passed it over to Everett, who thanked him. Orion finally collapsed back in his chair and leaned forward. Outside, the snow continued to fall from the sky.

"I don't know. I don't want to seem pathetic," Orion confessed.

"How many things do we do in this life, just so people don't think we're lame or dumb or pathetic?" Everett asked, arching an eyebrow.

"I'm in the public eye, dude," Orion stated. "Everyone looks at me and talks about what I'm doing. A million tweets will be sent about what happens today, probably more. It's enough to make my brain break."

"Okay. You're right. I can't ever really put myself in your shoes," Everett said.

Orion made heavy eye contact with him for a long moment. "I appreciate you trying, though, man. Really. I do. It's a rare thing in this world."

Chapter Twenty-One

The guests began to arrive for pre-wedding drinks around three in the afternoon. As far as Charlotte knew, Ursula remained in her suite, drinking bubbly champagne and crying to her mother about "the state of the world" and "how hard it was to be a celebrity." Naturally, Charlotte couldn't poke any holes into those arguments. She imagined it was rather difficult. Still, it annoyed her that this was meant to be her big break, she had dragged all her family members into this mess, and now they stood, almost all of them, in a big and beautifully decorated ballroom, wondering what was supposed to happen next.

Lola appeared beside her and arched her brow. "So Christine says she was just standing on the Joseph Sylvia Beach? Looking at the water?"

"In her wedding dress," Charlotte affirmed. "Yep."

"Is she out of her mind?"

"I think so," Charlotte said, giving her cousin a nod.

"That's too bad." Lola waved a hand toward the bartender on the far end of the ballroom, then put two fingers up. After a pause, there was a pop of a champagne bottle and the sound of glasses being filled. "Well, while she stews over her decisions, I guess that leaves the rest of us time to drink up," she said.

Charlotte laughed. "I wanted to be clear-headed for the ceremony and the party, but what the heck? Who knows what will happen next."

When the bartender arrived with their drinks, almost everyone else—Claire, Amanda, Susan, Scott, Tommy, Zach, and Christine—demanded their own glasses. The bartender hustled back and returned with a number of champagne bottles.

When everyone had a drink in their hand and Audrey had a little glass of bubbly water, Charlotte lifted her glass toward them.

"I want to thank all of you for your help over the past few weeks. I couldn't have done it without you. I don't know what will happen in the next few hours, but I guess, beyond anything, we can get drunk."

Everyone laughed and cheered and drank down their first of probably many glasses. At that moment, the doors burst open, and the sound of clicking cameras out near the curb filled the air.

"They've arrived," Christine said ominously.

And so they had.

Charlotte had never been particularly fascinated with the idea of being famous. In her mind, some of the best parts of being alive happened outside the allure of the camera. They were the in-betweens: Jason, delivering her a morning cup of coffee and a soft kiss on the forehead, for example, or Rachel, scratching her back when she couldn't quite reach.

As the celebrities, the same from last night and several more who had only just arrived on the island that afternoon, poured into the ballroom, they feasted on the view of the immaculate ballroom with eyes that seemed to know how many

Instagram likes this kind of party would get them. They posed with one another near the Christmas trees, puffing out their lips for each photo and sucking in their tummies. Charlotte eyed Rachel for a second, praying that watching these girls perform like this wouldn't change her own opinion about her body. She was beautiful, just the way she was, and always would be.

In the midst of the sea of celebrities, friends, and family of the bride and groom, Everett appeared. He wore this goofy grin that was no less attractive than his normal one, and he lifted his camera to snap several photos of the Sheridan and Montgomery clan as he approached.

"Look at you guys. You're hardly working at all," he teased.

"Not much to do," Christine said. "Zach's hard at work on the meal, but the rest of us are lying in wait to see if there's going to be a wedding at all."

Everett peered out at the crowd. "There's going to be something. I don't know if it'll be a wedding. But it'll be something."

"How did it go with Orion?" Charlotte asked.

"He poured me a drink of whiskey," Everett said with a laugh. "And me and the boys from the basketball team had a few really heartfelt conversations about life. To be honest with you, it was one of the stranger afternoons of my life."

"I'm right there with you on that one," Charlotte replied.

"Have you seen Ursula?" Everett asked.

The words basically summoned her.

Suddenly, Ursula herself, this gorgeous creature in a wedding gown with such fine beaded detail that it had taken the designer several months of his life to create, appeared in the doorway of the ballroom. Her hair was whipped around, a bit wild from her stint on the beach, but it looked as though someone—probably her mother—had touched up her hair and make-up as much as possible.

As Ursula was the most famous one of all of them, the people in the ballroom turned toward her and cheered. Ursula didn't give them any kind of smile. She looked on the verge of collapsing.

Instead, she reached out to grab a completely full champagne bottle from a tray of a passing server. The server blinked at her in shock but stepped away quickly as Ursula lifted the champagne bottle in the air. She looked a lot like Mel Gibson in *Braveheart*, Charlotte thought. Ready to lead the charge.

"I have an announcement to make!" Ursula cried out to the crowd before her.

Nobody spoke. Charlotte's stomach clenched.

"The wedding is off!" Ursula finished before knocking her head back and drinking the champagne straight from the bottle. Again, silence filled the room until she finished and swallowed. "But that doesn't mean we can't party!" she continued.

At this, every single person—including the Sheridan and Montgomery clan—roared.

"Wooo!" Audrey cried, wrapping her hand around her mouth to make it louder.

Charlotte burst into laughter. Tears fell down her cheeks. What the heck? After all she had been through? Had it come to this? Beside her, Everett continued to take as many photos as possible. When she turned toward him, she said, "What's the use? It's not like *Wedding Today* will feature the photos, right? I mean, the wedding is off."

Everett shook his head, his smile widening. "Actually, Charlotte, I think *Wedding Today* will happily take these photos. This wedding? It's going to go down in history. It'll make the magazine sell millions of copies. And you? You'll be known as the wedding planner behind it. I mean, look at what you did here. This ballroom, that dining hall over across the way? The décor is brilliant. The wedding would have been wonderful. And you did your job brilliantly!"

"But nobody will ever see it," Charlotte said, feeling foolish about her own sadness.

Everett shrugged. "You know that nothing is quite as good as we build it up in our heads to be."

Charlotte didn't know whether to laugh or cry now. She shook with emotion, but still wore a huge smile. She thought back to her own wedding to Jason—how she had built it up so much, but it had actually just been a tiny affair, a gathering of friends and family. She thought back to every staged moment, the things they had photographed, and the holidays they had shared. None of it had been exactly what she had ever planned for. And in that fact, she'd had a life to be grateful for.

"All right, team," Charlotte said, whipping around to grin at her family. "You heard the lady. Let's party!"

Chapter Twenty-Two

The party took on a new dimension after Ursula's announcement.

Charlotte hadn't seen anything like it, not in all her years of party-planning or even when she had visited girl-friends off the island at various college parties. The booze flowed; the gorgeous people fought and danced and laughed; Zach put out appetizer round after appetizer round and managed to only get into a few little spats with his servers.

"That's the most incredible part of all of this," Christine said to Charlotte in the corridor after they had both fixed their lipstick in the bathroom. "Zach? Not fighting that much? I mean, the man is a hothead."

Charlotte laughed.

"Ah, but I love him. So much. I hope when we finally get married, he lets someone else do the cooking, though," Christine continued. "I don't know if he trusts anyone else."

Dinner was served in the dining hall. Charlotte stuffed another chair at the family table to allow Everett to sit with them, and the two of them got lost in banter and good wine as the courses flowed out of the kitchen. Occasionally, Charlotte turned her eyes toward Ursula, who sat with her best friends, still in her wedding dress, and laughed and gossiped as if this was just any other day. What went through her head? Did she regret calling it all off?

But the air in the room didn't reek of regret. It was cinnamon, simmering with smells of roasted pork, potatoes, and all the fixings, including croissants and pies. Christine asked if she should pull out the wedding cake just to be featured, and Charlotte said, "Sure. What the heck! You created such a beautiful masterpiece. Let's not let it go to waste." When the cake was wheeled out, Ursula posed near it as a joke, and everyone laughed and snapped multiple photos. Charlotte heard more than one person ask who had made the cake. At this, she walked up and slipped one of Christine's cards into their hands. Christine deserved all the fame in the world.

Sometime around nine that evening, Charlotte found Everett near the coat room. Her heart lurched as she asked, "You aren't going, are you?"

"No. Not at all. I can't miss the rest of whatever this is," he said with a big smile. "I just wanted to get some air. It looks like it started snowing again."

Charlotte watched as Everett slipped on that massive coat, the one that had belonged to her Uncle Wes. "You really do look like you belong here," she told him. "No longer that west coast guy who arrived only days ago."

"Funny how things change," he said with a laugh as he looked down at his boots.

Charlotte grabbed her coat and headed out onto the porch with Everett. The snow fell softly, lit only by the moon. It was such a beautiful night.

"I wonder what will happen next in their lives," Everett said.

"I don't know. They're still young. They have everything ahead of them," Charlotte said.

"I wonder if they ever really loved each other," Everett said. "Or if it was all a lie they told themselves."

Charlotte shivered. "I think love is a beautiful answer to something. I don't know what the question is, exactly, but..." She trailed off and then forced herself to say, "I was married for about twenty years. My husband passed away last year in a fishing accident. For a long time, I thought I wouldn't live through it. I woke up every day in that bed alone, and I thought —what's the point?"

As she said the words, Charlotte realized that she hadn't explained her situation to anyone since it had happened. Everyone in her life had either known about it or not gotten close enough to her to find out.

"I don't know why I'm telling you this," Charlotte said, suddenly feeling a bit embarrassed about sharing too much. He hadn't even asked her about her situation, so why did she tell him that?

"I want to know this stuff," Everett said softly as he turned to look at her.

Charlotte's heart grew warm. She was reminded of that Grinch, whose heart outgrew his chest.

"You don't have to," Charlotte said. "I know this isn't your life. You're just a visitor. But..."

Everett shrugged. "But isn't it nice to be seen?"

Charlotte nodded as she looked at him.

But before she could answer, someone near the far end of the porch called her name.

Charlotte and Everett turned quickly to find Orion and Ursula.

Ursula was still dressed in her wedding dress; Orion had donned his tux.

They stood awkwardly, like young adults who had just been caught doing something wrong.

"Everett," Orion said in greeting.

"Orion," Everett nodded. "Hello, Ursula."

Ursula turned her eyes toward Charlotte. They glowed beautifully. "Charlotte, we've had a long conversation about today."

Finally.

"And we want to get married after all," Orion confessed.

What?

"But we don't want to do it in front of all those people," Ursula said. "I hardly even know most of them. O and I are almost always in the spotlight. It's our instinct to be in front of people. But what if that isn't the best way? What if the only way to step forward in marriage is to be by ourselves?"

Charlotte could hardly believe what she'd just heard.

Beside Ursula, Orion gave a firm nod. "Maybe you know somewhere we could go? A little church, or..."

"There's a little chapel," Charlotte said. "It's not far."

"A chapel. How quaint," Ursula said.

At first, Charlotte thought Ursula was being sarcastic. What would an LA actress want with a little chapel and nobody to watch?

But her eyes reflected just how certain she was of this new idea.

"Will you two come? Be our witnesses?" Orion asked with pleading eyes.

Charlotte's heart hammered within her chest. She blinked up at Everett, who looked just as shocked as she felt, and they both finally smiled at one another.

"Of course we will," she said. "I'll call the pastor and have him meet us there. Everett?"

"I'll call a few taxis," Everett said. "We'll be there in no time."

* * *

Ursula's wedding dress did, in fact, take up most of the back of one of the taxis. Charlotte thanked Everett for ordering a second one, which brought the two of them, along with the pastor, over to the little chapel. The pastor had performed a number of wedding ceremonies at that very chapel, and he even had a key. He snapped on the lights as the four of them stood awkwardly toward the back of the chapel.

"All right. I'll head up there. Orion, you come along with me," the pastor said. "Our witnesses? Take your seat. And Ursula? I think you know what to do."

There wasn't music. At first, Charlotte's instinct was to put something on, something to fill the silence. But as Ursula walked up the little aisle of the chapel, her eyes heavy with tears, Charlotte realized that their emotions were too powerful; they required nothing else as a backdrop.

"You look beautiful," Orion breathed, taking her hands in his.

"You look so handsome," Ursula said.

She sounded different in these moments. Charlotte compared it to all the movies she had seen with Ursula acting in them. This was clearly the real Ursula, the one she kept only for Orion.

Everett reached across and gripped Charlotte's hand as the two of them read their vows. Charlotte didn't dare look at Everett; she knew she would burst into tears. With every breath she took, she knew she was falling for him.

And she couldn't.

He was going to leave.

She couldn't let herself go there.

When Ursula and Orion kissed for the first time as husband and wife, Everett and Charlotte stood and clapped and beamed at the couple. They turned and grinned back, again looking much more like young adults than world-famous millionaires. Charlotte supposed that's what love was, in the end: just a couple of people taking on the world together.

They had paid the taxis to wait to bring them back to the mansion. In the taxi, the pastor heaved a sigh and said, "I'm going to bed. This is much later than I planned on staying awake today. You said the wedding would be at four in the afternoon!"

Charlotte laughed. "I'm so sorry, Pastor, but the plans changed. We had no control."

"If God wills it," the pastor said. "I suppose you're right."

Back in the reception ballroom, Charlotte and Everett re-entered the fold of Charlotte's family to intense speculation.

"Where have you two been?" Lola hissed at them.

"What do you mean?" Everett said, his eyes sparkling with secrecy. "We just stepped outside on the porch."

"Yeah. Right," Lola snorted.

"You can't get anything past Mom," Audrey said, stepping up, her hand wrapped around another croissant. "She sees everything. Luckily, I managed to get pregnant out of state."

"You always have to bring it back to that, don't you?" Lola said, rolling her eyes.

That moment, Ursula and Orion burst into the ballroom, their hands latched together and their smiles enormous. Everyone stopped talking. Even the DJ quit the beats.

"WE GOT MARRIED!" Ursula cried out suddenly. Orion tore toward her, bent her backward, and kissed her the way all women want to be kissed. When he brought his lips away from hers, he held his nose against hers tenderly.

It was enough to make your heart break.

Immediately, the ballroom buzzed with activity.

Photos had to be taken; Instagram Lives had to be filmed; tweets had to be sent; people had to tell everyone else about their opinions—like, *I can't believe they actually went through with it. They're terrible for each other,* or *I KNEW they were doing that. I figured they would sneak off and then make a whole big scene. That's so Ursula. If you knew her the way I know her, you'd think that, too.*

But honestly, none of it mattered. The only thing that mattered in these final hours of the reception was that—heck— Charlotte had done it. She had put on one of the more memorable weddings of the past twenty, thirty, forty years. She had pulled it off but not without a hitch.

"Sit back, now, baby, because you're finally done," Everett said teasingly.

Baby? He's joking, obviously, but...

I want him to call me that again.

Charlotte laughed, forcing herself not to take the whole thing so seriously. "Let's have another drink, shall we?"

"Only if you dance with me," Everett said.

"That's forward of you, thinking that I might want to dance with you," Charlotte said.

Everett shrugged. "I figure it's the kind of day to take chances."

"Maybe you're right." She grinned and set her glass to the side just as a slow song came through the speakers. "Let's get this over with."

"Sorry to put you through so much torture," he joked.

Charlotte hadn't danced with a man since two years before Jason's death when they had attended a wedding of one of their high school friends.

At the time, she had taken it for granted, just the way most women who had been married for what seemed like forever took such things for granted.

Now, with Everett's arms around her, she shivered.

She wanted to tell him how weird it was for her.

But he did it first.

"I haven't danced with a woman like this in a long time," he told her. "I don't even know when it would have been. Ten years ago? Prom even?"

Charlotte laughed. "Why has it been so long?"

"I guess I've never bothered to get close enough to a woman to want to dance with her like this," Everett explained.

His eyes meant business.

Like he wanted to be close to her.

"Am I out of practice?" he asked, interjecting her thoughts.

Charlotte shook her head. "I think you're doing okay. Maybe a B or a B+."

"I'll take it. That's a passing grade," he said, smiling down at her.

The song ended, and then, several songs later, the night ended. One of the actresses from a recently acclaimed film ran outside to throw up in the snow, and another guy audibly broke up with his girlfriend in the corner. Ursula and Orion had spent the majority of the last hour stuffing Christine's cake in one another's face and making out with reckless abandon.

"I think it's safe to say this party went off the rails," Christine said, her eyes on the couple.

"It started off the rails. I don't know where we are now," Everett said. "How did Zach hold up, by the way?"

"I thought he was going to throw a knife earlier, but now he and the servers are partying in the kitchen," Christine said. "The man knows how to cook, though. He outdid himself today. And he says he'll take us on vacation next week. I could use a beach somewhere. Especially before the baby comes." She beamed at Audrey.

Charlotte and Everett hovered out on the porch and watched the guests as they filtered back into their taxis and limos, returning to the hotels and inns across the island. Those who stayed on at the mansion had already headed up to their rooms, and the ballroom was slowly clearing out.

"This was one of the wildest weekends of my life," Everett said. His eyes caught hers.

Charlotte's heart thudded. This was the moment, wasn't it? The moment every girl waited for.

"I hate that I have to leave tomorrow," Everett said.

"Los Angeles awaits," Charlotte said.

Everett paused for a moment, then swept forward and delivered a perfect kiss—the kind of kiss that made Charlotte weak in the knees. Her eyes closed, and the world slowed down around her. She no longer heard the screaming celebrities; she no longer remembered the stress of the day.

The only thing that mattered was this moment.

And all too soon, the kiss ended. Charlotte watched in shock and awe as Everett nodded and said, "I'll see you when I see you," and walked out across the snow, ducking into the taxi furthest away.

Charlotte was sure she would never see him again.

But he had given her something she hadn't thought she would ever feel again.

Now, she had hope.

Chapter Twenty-Three

Everett stood at the magazine and newspapers stand in LAX the following evening.

In his right hand, he still held onto Charlotte's Uncle Wes's massive winter coat from the seventies. He had only realized that mistake when he had been halfway through his drive from Falmouth to Boston, midway through the day. "Shoot," he had muttered as he'd stripped it off at airport security.

"Where you headed?" the woman at security had asked him.

"LA," he'd told her.

"I guess you won't need that coat all the way over there," she'd said with a funny smile.

"No. I guess not."

Now, his heart ached with the memories of the last few days.

It had been a whirlwind, from that first chance encounter of Lola and Christine at one of the local bars to the gorgeous

Thanksgiving dinner celebration at the Sheridan house, then on through the weekend, until that final kiss the night before.

He hadn't braved contacting Charlotte that morning. She had told him about her husband—something he hadn't expected her to do, as it was clearly very difficult for her to talk about. He hadn't fully known if that was some kind of invitation? Some kind of, *I'm interested in you, and I want you to hear my story?* There was no way to say.

On the flight, it had occurred to Everett that since Charlotte had been married for around twenty years, she probably hadn't dated much. Could he attribute all his confusion around it to the fact that she just hadn't known what to say or do?

His eyes scanned the newspapers until he dragged one out of the Sunday *New York Times*, still one of the most sought-after newspapers in a world that was much more fascinated with online publications these days. He bought the newspaper from the guy at the counter and sat on the bench nearby. People in front of him walked down the hallway quickly, their eyes focused, their bags dragging behind them. For whatever reason, Everett didn't feel any big rush to get back to his Silver Lake apartment.

Oscar-Winning Actress and NBA Basketball Player Tie the Knot in Secret Ceremony

The article was in the Society section. There was so much to say that the writer had managed to fill an entire page. A photo that was nearly identical to the one Everett had taken—when Ursula and Orion had burst back into the reception after their official ceremony at the chapel—graced the page.

This wasn't your average, everyday marriage between two millionaires on Martha's Vineyard.

I know it doesn't sound like it should be any different. Maybe, on paper, it wasn't. There were certainly thousand-dollar bottles of champagne, gorgeous details on the Christmas trees, a string quintet, celebrities from twenty different countries and fifty different films and TV shows, and several music performers with top Spotify ratings.

This reporter assumed that it would be just another wedding.

But it wasn't. In fact, for the majority of Saturday, most of the guests assumed the entire wedding was canceled. Ursula Pennington herself stormed into the reception area and announced it, then immediately downed a bottle of champagne.

It was strange for Everett to read the events back to himself. It felt almost as though the things that had happened had been a part of someone else's life. He skimmed down a bit more before he caught sight of Charlotte's name.

Charlotte Hamner, a remarkable newfound force in the wedding industry, did the best she could with what she had. Her décor was immaculate; the parties were stunning. But beyond this, a source close to the actress herself states that Charlotte brought Ursula and Orion to a nearby chapel for the ceremony itself after they decided to marry after all. It's this commitment to unique detail, according to some, that led Ursula to hire the woman in the first place.

I'm sure this isn't the last time this reporter will write about the likes of the wedding planner, Charlotte Hamner.

Everett grinned inwardly as he folded up the newspaper and tucked it under his arm.

Outside, Everett called for a Lyft car and darted into the back seat, still holding onto that huge coat. The Lyft driver was a California guy through and through, and he scoffed at the coat. "Where were you? I hope you went skiing."

Everett gave a half-answer about a job he had to do out east. He let his head roll back on the car seat as the vehicle rolled toward Silver Lake. For reasons he couldn't fully name, the place looked much different than it had before he'd left—as though his brief stint out east had left his eyes permanently changed. When he closed them, he saw snow behind his eyelids.

What was that about?

Back in his apartment, he received a text from the girl he had been seeing on and off over the previous month or so. He thought back to their few nights together, how stunted the conversation had been. He made the decision to end it.

Compared to what he had built with Charlotte, it had been next to nothing, anyway.

He sat at his kitchen table and scanned through his phone.

It was the first time in several days that he gave full attention to other people's lives, which was also a difference for him.

People in California were normally looking in on one another, always trying to "win" the situation with a better life.

Back on Martha's Vineyard, Everett hadn't considered anyone else's life once.

He had just actually liked where he'd been, who he had been around.

But what did that mean?

He couldn't just decide to move there out of the blue. That was crazy. It was the kind of thing Charlotte—or women like Charlotte—would turn their noses at.

Everett busied himself with the photographs he had taken the previous days at the rehearsal dinner and the wedding. It took a number of hours to edit the "keepers" properly and send them off to his editor, who wrote back almost instantly.

These are incredible, Everett—but not as wild as that wedding sounds like it was. *The Times* broke it. Apparently, they had someone on the inside?

At this, Everett leafed again for the newspaper to read the byline.

He laughed to himself.

Lola Sheridan

What were the chances? And when had she found the chance to write it and send it off? Early that morning? Had she stayed up all night?

The Sheridan women were certainly something else.

Anyway, I think we'll have a spread on this in the next issue. Do you think we should include more about the wedding planner? There's been buzz about her, even after we featured her in that Q&A the other day. Let me know. You probably met her?

Everett dropped his head back and blinked at the ceiling. His sink started leaking, a horrible drip-drip-drip against the bottom, and he bolted up to turn the handle all the way back down again.

He hadn't gotten her number.

But probably, she had a website, right?

He found the *Wedding Today* website and went immediately to the Q&A with Charlotte Hamner. Sure enough, her website was listed. He found it, then found that she didn't have a direct email or phone number, just a contact box.

He had to fill out the contact box to get to her, just like every other bride in the world.

And he felt like a complete idiot doing it.

Hey Charlotte,

It's Everett.

I realized I'm an idiot and didn't get your number or email or anything.

My editor wants to include more info about you in the article about the event. Is that okay with you?

As I'm filling this out, I realize that my editor probably already has your details and has already emailed you directly with this exact question.

So I'm feeling more and more stupid as I write this.

To put it frankly, I liked meeting you. Now that I'm back on the west coast, sitting here with your Uncle Wes's enormous winter coat, I realize I liked meeting you more than I like meeting other people.

Don't know what I want you to do with that information.

I guess I just want you to know that, just in case.

Everett stared at that cursor at the bottom of the little contact box for a long time. It was almost ten at night, which meant it was one in the morning over there. She would get it in the cold light of Monday morning.

Great.

But there was no way he could turn back now.

He clicked his mouse on the SEND button and then watched the box transform to a:

Thank you for contacting Charlotte Hamner! She will get back to you soon and can't wait to help you transform your wedding dreams into a reality.

Everett changed into his boxers and tried to get some sleep in his bed, which he had bought used from another friend who'd wised up and returned to Seattle after a year of LA. He flopped around in the bed for a little while until he whacked his hand to the side and gripped his phone. He heaved a sigh, then began to drum up another message.

Apparently, there was a lot on his mind.

Hey Mom. I wanted to apologize for missing Thanksgiving. I missed your apple pie (and your company) more than I can say. I hope we can mend our relationship soon. I love you.

The minute he sent it, the app showed his mother writing back.

Apparently, he wasn't the only one sleepless on this Sunday night.

Before she finished writing, she called him.

Everett answered on the first ring.

"Mom?"

"Everett." Her voice sounded heavy with tears. "I'm so glad you wrote to me."

"Mom, I really am sorry."

"It's okay. We missed you a lot. Your brother's kids kept asking about you."

"I'll be back to see them soon. To see all of you. I promise."

His mother held the silence for a while. They had just always been quiet people. "Maybe you could come this week?"

Everett considered it. He didn't have another event to photograph till Thursday, and the flight to Seattle was just a couple of hours.

After everything he had seen between the Sheridans and the Montgomerys, all he wanted in the world was a family who loved each other, one that knew how to forgive.

"I'll get on the first flight tomorrow," he told her.

"Thank you, Everett. I'll make another apple pie, just for you."

Chapter Twenty-Four

Charlotte appeared at the Sheridan house that Monday morning with her head full of adrenaline. Somehow, knowing that that message was in her inbox, she had gotten Rachel ready for school. Somehow, she'd managed to shower herself, feed herself a yogurt, and check the news for even more information about the Ursula and Orion wedding.

Somehow she had done all that.

But now, she had to check this message.

She entered through the back door without knocking. It was still pretty early, which meant that Christine was probably over at the Bistro, Lola was probably still sleeping, and Susan was probably up at the Sunrise Cove Inn, operating the desk. Charlotte would take whoever was around for moral support.

Message from Everett R.

As if there were any other Everett Rs in the world.

Actually, she told herself that if there *was* another Everett R, and he was the one to contact her on her website, she would scream into a pillow for a full hour.

To her surprise, Lola, Christine, Audrey, and Susan all sat around the kitchen table, drinking coffee and nibbling on croissants.

"Aren't you a sight for sore eyes!" Lola called.

Charlotte nearly burst into tears but managed to hold it back and laugh instead. Funny how similar those actions were.

"We were just talking about you," Susan said. She burst to her feet and walked toward the coffee pot, where she poured Charlotte a mug and passed it over the counter. "You look like you got at least a little sleep?"

"I did, yeah. Still exhausted from the weekend," Charlotte said.

"I don't think that will go away very quickly," Christine said with a laugh.

Audrey stood and grabbed another chair for Charlotte, placing it between herself and Lola. "How are you feeling? The entire internet exploded after what happened over the weekend."

"Yeah. People keep memeing it. Especially that photo of Ursula coming in all drunk and announcing the wedding was off," Christine said.

"What's a meme again?" Susan said from the kitchen.

"Don't worry about it, Aunt Susie. The less you know about the meme world, the better," Audrey said.

"I guess I'll ask Amanda, then," Susan said sarcastically, returning to her seat.

"Anyway. Have you heard from Ursula?" Audrey asked. "She keeps posting videos from her and Orion's trip to the Bahamas. It's beautiful." She turned her phone around to show Ursula and Orion out on a white strip of sand, drinking fruity drinks. "The woman is a menace, for sure, but she knows how to party. I can appreciate that."

"Ha. Yes, she wrote to me yesterday," Charlotte said.

"And?"

"She just thanked me again for everything we did. I don't know. She seems like a good person. She just lives a very different kind of life than the rest of us," Charlotte explained.

"That's true. And the money came through all right?"

Charlotte had, in fact, been paid handsomely. She had never felt more comfortable in her life. She nodded, feeling her cheeks burn.

"Then why do you seem so sad?" Audrey asked.

At that moment, another person entered through the back door. They spun around to find Claire ambling through, a big smile on her face.

"I checked your house and figured you would be here," Claire said.

Charlotte was so grateful to see her sister. She latched her arms around her and tugged her down.

"We were just asking Aunt Charlotte why she's sad," Audrey said, splaying her hand across her pregnant belly.

"You're sad? Why are you sad?" Claire asked, furrowing her brow. She grabbed a croissant from the table as Susan rose to pour her a cup of coffee.

"I'm not, really," Charlotte said.

"I see it written all over your face," Audrey said. "You look like my roommate last year when that frat boy broke her heart."

"I know why. It's because of Everett," Lola said.

Charlotte's nostrils flared.

"That's it. It's so obvious now," Christine said.

"What happened on Saturday?" Claire asked.

"Nothing really," Charlotte said.

"But you two actually saw the wedding between Orion and Ursula," Lola said.

"Sure. We did. It was kind of a miracle. We were just out watching the snow."

"Just out watching the snow," Susan said, teasing her. "Come on. Something must have happened."

Charlotte felt just as she had a million years ago when she had first kissed Jason, and she'd felt her life change for good.

"I don't know. We kissed, I guess."

"You kissed!" Every single woman at the table howled with excitement.

"I don't know what to say. You kissed Everett, and then you let him just fly out west?" Claire demanded.

"Oh my gosh, Claire. I'm a grown woman. I can kiss people and let it be over," Charlotte said, giving her sister a nasty glare.

I mean, I wish I was like that.

"The way you looked at him was different," Claire said. "You looked at him like he meant something to you. I don't think that comes around every day."

Charlotte shrugged. "It doesn't matter, does it? It's a good story. A great one, even. But he lives on the west coast, and I live here." She swallowed, anticipating the world collapsing when she said the next bit of information. "The thing is, I think he wrote to me through my website last night. And I'm freaking out."

Yep. Every single woman at the table burst into yelps and exclamations. It was like sitting at the lunch table in middle school.

"Chill out, you guys!" Charlotte cried out. She was starting to get annoyed with each of them.

"Read the message. Right. Now," Claire demanded.

"You heard your sister," Lola said. "I always listen to my sister when she tells me what to do."

"That's obviously a lie," Susan said with a laugh. "But I hope you'll read it to us, anyway."

Charlotte did. She read the entire note aloud, and then she read it privately while the girls yelled and screamed about it.

"You have got to be kidding me," Claire cried.

"*I realize I liked meeting you more than I like meeting other people,*" Lola quoted. "Phew. That is a lot to think about."

"It is, isn't it?" Charlotte breathed.

"But you can't just let this die," Christine ordered. "Seriously. He's after you. He wants to see you again. And right now —I don't know if you know this or not—you have a little bit of extra cash floating around."

Charlotte's heart jumped. "I can't. What about Rachel?"

"Any one of us can watch Rachel while you're gone," Christine said. "The bistro is slow as ever right now since it's winter. Zach and I could stay at your house while you're away as we practice becoming parents. Besides. When was the last time you had a vacation?"

Everyone agreed that it was insane that Charlotte hadn't had a single break.

Tied up in all this, Charlotte could hear what they really meant. *Even if this doesn't work out, you deserve a break after everything you went through. Your husband died, and you just kept going.*

You almost didn't make it, but you did.

Charlotte bit hard on her lower lip.

"Okay. Okay, okay. I'll ask him." She grinned broadly, realizing how crazy and spontaneous this was—and loving the feeling of it. "And if he rejects me?"

"He lives on the other side of the continent. Who cares?" Lola said.

This was the perfect response.

Chapter Twenty-Five

Charlotte drummed up the courage to write Everett back that afternoon.

She sat at the Sunrise Cove Bistro with a glass of wine and wrote and rewrote the message until she drank through a whole glass of wine and needed to order a second. Outside, snow fluttered down, uninterested in letting up. Although she loved it, she couldn't help but imagine Everett's sunny life out in LA.

He had seen her life. He had met her father and her mother, her cousins, her sisters, her daughter, and one of her brothers.

In actuality, she knew so very little about him.

"You look frustrated." Zach walked over from the kitchen area as he dried his hands on a towel.

Charlotte sighed. "Is it that obvious?"

Zach laughed. "Anything I can help you with? You got me one of the best gigs of my career. I would love to pay you back somehow."

Charlotte shook her head. "Maybe just another glass of wine. I need liquid courage to send this out."

"I'm on it," Zach said. He disappeared for a second and then returned with a bottle of wine. "It's really coming down out there. I can't help but think of Ursula and Orion, all the way in the Bahamas. Do you think they'll stay together?"

"Maybe. I don't know," Charlotte said truthfully. "I guess nobody ever knows what will happen next."

"Nobody knows that more than me right now. Every day that Audrey's delivery date creeps closer, I get a little more nervous. Christine and I have talked about adopting other children of our own afterward and—" He tilted his head thoughtfully. "I guess you can never go backward, so it's always better to go forwards."

Charlotte loved the sentiment.

She only hoped she had the strength to follow her gut.

Finally, she settled on a half-decent message back.

Everett,

I've gotten about two hundred inquiries this past day on my website.

Glad I pieced through them and found yours.

I wanted to say that I am glad I met you, too.

And also...

What are you doing this weekend?

I've heard California is sunny this time of year.

Or is it sunny year-round?

This girl hasn't traveled much.

Charlotte

Chapter Twenty-Six

Everett's mother's house was the same house Everett had grown up in.

Just as he remembered it, it brimmed with the glorious smell of cinnamon-baked apples.

He found his mother seated in her favorite reading chair, with a book stretched out on her lap and her head tilted up toward the sun. Her eyes were closed, and her lips were parted just slightly, proof that she had drowsed off.

Everett wasn't the kind of guy to wake up his mother.

He would wait and let her sleep.

He sat on the sofa across from her and reached for his phone to check his email. Again, his editor celebrated the photographs he had sent. He also assigned him a number of events and weddings in the future, which Everett would accept when he got his head around them. Just then, he had a number of things to take care of.

He had to repair his relationship with his family.

As he tapped through his email, he noticed that the SPAM folder held a familiar name.

Charlotte Hamner.

His heart jumped into his throat. He glanced up toward his mother, then back at his phone.

She had answered him.

He read the message.

Then, he read it again.

Then, he stood from the couch and paced back and forth in his mother's living room until the oven timer blared, waking his mother from her sleep and him from his reckless imagination.

She wants to visit me in California.

She wants to see this through.

"Everett?" his mother said, her voice creaking. "Is that really you?"

She stood slowly, peering at him with eyes that seemed still half-asleep.

"It's me, Mom," Everett said. He gripped her hands, which seemed more like paper than they had been even a year ago. "I made it."

His mother flung herself at him and wrapped her arms around his thick chest. The oven timer continued to scream, but she didn't seem to care at all. Her body shook with tears.

I'll never make her feel like this again.

I will be a better son.

I'll visit her more often.

I'll be what she needs.

Finally, she dropped back and gave her cheeks a few light smacks. "Oh, darling, the oven! The pie!" She raced toward the oven and flung it open to reveal a beautiful pie. Delicately, she placed it on top of the stove and beamed down at it.

"Look at that," Everett said with a big smile.

"It's your favorite," she said, smiling.

"You are the best, Mom. Thank you."

* * *

Everett explained the situation with Charlotte to his mother as they dug into their warm slices of apple pie. Vanilla ice cream melted over the top as he spoke of her, of her daughter, and of the husband she had lost.

"I can't explain it, Mom. She just seems different than the other women I've met."

"Marriage material," his mother said softly.

"I don't know. I don't know. It's way too soon to know." Everett sighed. "But I've never thought that I ever wanted to marry. And now, I have this feeling that if I found the right person..."

"You would find the space in your heart," his mother finished the sentence for him.

"Exactly," he said, pointing his fork at her.

His mother reached across the table and gripped his hand. They studied one another for a long time.

"I hope you find a way to love her—or whoever you end up with—as much as your father loved me," she said. "If so, she will have the greatest happiness."

Chapter Twenty-Seven

Charlotte was full-on freaking out.

Everett had formally invited her to California that Saturday, a whole week after the wedding.

She stood over her empty suitcase on Thursday evening, her hands on her hips, while Claire, Rachel, Abby, and Gail hovered behind her. They planned to help her pack and help her decide what to wear in this city of sunshine. Slowly, Claire helped her pick through her summer dresses, choosing the ones that Charlotte didn't have any overly intense memories in and splaying them on the bed.

"Oh yeah. You look hot in that one, Mom," Rachel said, pointing to the bright red one Claire held in her arms.

"Hot? At forty-one?" Charlotte said, eyeing her daughter.

Rachel, Abby, and Gail nodded, bug-eyed.

"Are you kidding?" Gail demanded. "All the Sheridan and Montgomery girls are hotter after forty, it seems like."

"We're blessed with good genes," Abby affirmed.

Claire folded the dresses, skirts, and shirts they had chosen, while Charlotte was assigned to go through her underwear collection to pick out something appropriate. Her cheeks burned.

"I don't know. Maybe we're just going to be friends?" she said sheepishly.

"Right. And I'm the next Queen of England," Claire declared.

Charlotte pressed her lips together anxiously. "Then I think we're going to have to go shopping. Everything in this drawer is the kind of thing I wore as a married woman."

Claire marched over to investigate. After she clucked her tongue, she said, "Yep. This is basically what my drawer looks like, too. Lots and lots of holes and granny panties. Maybe I'll come with you? Spruce up my lingerie?"

"It'll be a bonding experience," Charlotte joked.

* * *

Charlotte had never been off the island without her husband, one of her friends, cousins, siblings, or one of her parents. Now, at age forty-one, she hugged her daughter goodbye and walked onto the ferry with her chin held high. She had always believed that you had to pretend you were confident; the rest came later.

All of life was a little bit like an act, anyway.

At the airport, she bought a cup of coffee and sat watching the planes as they ducked down, then eased back into the bright blue sky. It was early December, and the airport was decorated with cheery tinsel, Christmas trees, Santa Clauses, and ornaments hanging from the ceilings.

The plane to LA took about six hours.

During the last hour, she had to convince herself to keep breathing.

The woman seated beside her asked if she needed any water or a snack since she looked pale.

Charlotte didn't want to look anything but her best when she met Everett.

A little panicked, she rushed to the bathroom, smeared extra lipstick across both her lips and her upper cheeks, and pleaded with herself to act normal.

You went across the entire continent to meet a man you hardly know.

What makes you think this is the right thing to do?

Still, she needed it. Right?

She deserved it.

She had been through so much.

And Jason would have wanted her to move on.

When the plane landed, she closed her eyes and cupped her elbows and tried her best to talk to Jason, wherever he was.

I love you. You know I'll always love you. You know that every decision I make is for our daughter, Rachel.

I hope you know that no matter what new experiences I build with someone new, you'll still be a part of me.

I will never let you go. Not completely.

Charlotte waited for her luggage at the carousel and headed toward the pick-up zone. Outside the door, early December Los Angeles heat was a welcome feeling, like cozying into a nice sweater. She inhaled the strange air and then turned her head to find Everett standing next to a little red car with his arm extended.

He was so handsome. His black hair was curled wildly, and his blue eyes reflected the gorgeous California sun. He looked at her like she was the only woman in the world.

She walked toward him. The walk felt like it took forever. All her thoughts seemed to be one large mess in her head.

When she stood before him, she heaved a sigh, dropped her suitcase to the side, and placed her hands on her hips.

"I came all this way," she finally said as he studied her face. "Aren't you going to say hello?"

He didn't speak.

His hands extended over her cheeks as he kissed her.

Their eyes closed.

In the sky, planes flew toward the airstrip and back into the sky above.

Still, they kissed.

Charlotte's heart lifted into her throat.

She felt that they, too, could have flown away.

When their kiss broke, she gripped his hands and pressed her teeth into her lower lip.

Behind them, some guy who waited for Everett's car to get out of the way leaped out of the driver's side and hollered, "All right. That's enough! Some of us want to get home to see our families."

At that, Everett finally laughed, shrugged, and said, "Welcome to LA. What else did you expect?"

As they drove out toward Silver Lake, Charlotte splayed one hand out the window while she gripped Everett's with her left. The radio played songs they'd always known, with lyrics they sang along to. In these moments, she wasn't forty-one, or seventeen, or anyone, or anything she really recognized. She was just happy. And she was so grateful to find that it was still possible.

* * *

Next in the series

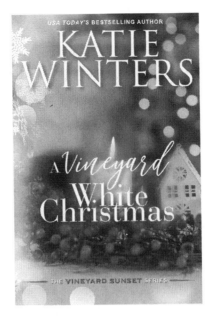

Other Books by Katie

The Vineyard Sunset Series

Secrets of Mackinac Island Series

Sisters of Edgartown Series

A Katama Bay Series

A Mount Desert Island Series

A Nantucket Sunset Series

Connect with Katie Winters

BookBub
Facebook
Newsletter

To receive exclusive updates from Katie Winters please sign up
to be on her Newsletter!
CLICK HERE TO SUBSCRIBE

Made in the USA
Middletown, DE
22 February 2023